The
ROAD
BACK

LIVING WITH A
PHYSICAL DISABILITY

Harriet Sir~~c~~f

D1523809

AN AUTHORS GUILD BACKINPRINT.COM EDITION

The Road Back:
Living with a Physical Disability
All Rights Reserved © 1993, 2000 by Harriet Sirof

AN AUTHORS GUILD BACKINPRINT.COM EDITION

Published by iUniverse.com, Inc.

For information address:
iUniverse.com, Inc.
620 North 48th Street, Suite 201
Lincoln, NE 68504-3467
www.iuniverse.com

Originally published by New Discovery Books

ISBN: 0-595-09071-0

Printed in the United States of America

FOR ALL OF US
WHO HAVE TRAVELED
THE ROAD BACK
AND FOR EVERYONE
WHO HELPED US
ALONG THE WAY.

CONTENTS

INTRODUCTION

Your life could change in a minute. A truck might skid on a wet road and slam into your car. You might be thrown off your skateboard into a wall. Or you might wake up one morning unable to see out of one eye. You could suddenly be disabled.

Without giving it much thought, able-bodied people may feel that those with disabilities are somehow "different." But if you developed a serious disease, you wouldn't suddenly become a different person. Whether you had a broken hip that healed in a few months or a broken neck that left you paralyzed, you would still be you. If a disease affected your walking or seeing or hearing or breathing, you would still be you. You might face problems you never dreamed you would have. You might have to work hard at getting well. Or you might have to learn to live with your disability. But being sick or disabled wouldn't stop you from feeling or caring or hoping or dreaming. It wouldn't make you less of a person. And that is the point of this book.

CHAPTER 1

Life Can Change in a Minute

H ere are some statistics:

- Every four seconds someone in the United States is injured in an accident. Every year 8,760,000 Americans are temporarily disabled, and 340,000 are permanently disabled by accidents. Nearly half the victims are under the age of 25. Accidents are the leading cause of teen deaths.

- **Spinal cord injuries** paralyze 7,800 Americans a year. The most common age at the time of injury is 19.

- **Multiple sclerosis (MS)** is a disease of the **nervous system.** Every week 200 new cases are diagnosed. Most are young adults. Twenty-five percent eventually need to use wheelchairs. There are 1.4 million Americans in wheelchairs today.

- More than 2 million students in the United States have diseases or **disabilities** that limit their school activities.

Behind these statistics are people. Trisha was 14 when a truck hit her family's car. Her father had picked her up after a party at her cousin's house. It was late, and the swish of the tires on the wet highway made her sleepy. She opened her seat belt, leaned back, and dozed. She didn't notice a large truck passing the car. She didn't see it skid. She didn't know she was in danger until she slammed into the dashboard. Because she hit her head on the windshield, all she remembered of the ambulance, the emergency room, and the operating room was the fright and the pain. When she woke up, she was tied down in a hospital bed after the operation that repaired her broken hip. She hurt everywhere. Her mother told her, "Don't try to move. Rest now. Everything will be all right." Trisha closed her eyes and went back to sleep.

At 16, Steven loved anything on wheels, anything that went fast. He couldn't wait to get his driver's license. Meanwhile, he made do with a skateboard and a racing bike. He was zipping along the waterside promenade on his skateboard when the accident happened. Because he'd turned to watch a fisherman pull in a big one, he was caught off balance when the skateboard wheels tangled in a discarded fishing line. He was thrown into the seawall, and a protruding stone caught him in the lower back. It was ages since he had fallen off his skateboard. Steven felt stupid lying on the ground, but he couldn't get up. He couldn't move.

Christopher developed strange symptoms while he was applying to college during his senior year of high school. Sometimes his legs felt heavy; other times his eyesight blurred. And he was always tired. His mother was worried and insisted he see their family doctor and an eye doctor. The eye doctor prescribed stronger glasses. The family doctor said Chris might have a pinched nerve, or it could all be stress. He told Chris not to worry so much about getting into college.

Chris's first-choice college accepted him, and he looked forward to going away to school. Then, one morning, he woke up blind in his right eye. The eye doctor sent him to a **neurologist,** a specialist in the diseases of the nervous system. The neurologist ordered a battery of tests. Chris's eye was fine by the time the test results came in. But that didn't change the diagnosis. He had multiple sclerosis.

Like most teens, Trisha, Steven, and Christopher took their healthy bodies for granted. In the past, being sick meant having a cold or flu and getting better in a few days. Now they had to deal with their bodies not doing what they expected. They had to cope with not getting better quickly.

Most people with a serious injury or illness go through a number of emotional stages. The first reaction is shock and confusion. They feel as if they were dropped into a foreign country without knowing the language or the customs or the way they are supposed to act. There is a rush of confused feelings: disbelief, fear, frustration, anger, guilt, self-pity, despair, numbness. All they can do is hang in there and try to make it through the next hours and days.

When the shock wears off, the next stage is usually denial. It is too painful to accept that life has changed, that there are things they can't do anymore. One boy tells himself, "I can't walk right now, but I'll get better soon." Or when a girl hears she has cancer, she thinks, "Doctors are wrong lots of times. They must be wrong about me because I don't feel that sick." Often parents can't bear to see their child in pain, so they, too, deny what has happened. And family and friends help the denial by telling stories about people with the same condition who were cured.

After a while, when the condition doesn't go away, denial stops working and grief and mourning set in. It's natural to mourn the loss of your healthy body and carefree life. Most people become depressed as well. Some give in to feeling hopeless and helpless. They curl up into a ball of misery and hide. Others get angry.

Anger and/or guilt usually go along with depression and grief. When life plays a dirty trick on you, you get mad. Sometimes people take their anger out on everyone around or blow up at every little thing. Or they look for someone to blame: the doctor who didn't spot the sickness sooner, the truck driver who skidded, the guy who threw away the fishing line. Sometimes they blame themselves, "If only I hadn't. . . ."

Gradually, most people begin to accept their disability. They learn how to live with it. It takes time, but they work out a new life-style. Although it didn't seem possible at the beginning, they learn to be happy again.

Adjusting to a disability isn't an orderly, step-by-step process of going through one stage after another. There isn't a week for shock, two weeks for denial, a month for mourning. Each person copes in his own way and at her own rate. Some skip a stage entirely, while others get stuck in being angry or depressed for a long time.

How someone reacts depends on how serious the injury or illness is and on whether it will get better, get worse, or stay the same. Hope helps. People with conditions that are expected to improve usually deny less and cope more quickly than those who won't get much better.

People with diseases that become progressively worse often go through shock, denial, and grief with every new symptom. Those who suffer permanent disabilities usually have the longest periods of denial and mourning. It is obviously easier to adjust to a cane than to a wheelchair, and asthma is usually less devastating than cancer.

But not always. One person will deal with a major disability with great courage, while another is completely thrown by a much less serious condition. What a person was like before the accident or illness makes a big difference in how he or she copes with it. After the shock wears off, most people react as they did to earlier problems in their lives. Depending on how they usually dealt with problems, they work at getting better or retreat into misery. Teens, who were in the process of changing from children into adults, may go back to acting babyish for a while. Or they may grow up in a hurry.

How successfully people rebuild their lives also depends on the help they get. Nobody can do it alone. Good medical care and an active rehabilitation program are very important. So is the love and support of family and friends.

Because Trisha, Steven, and Christopher had different kinds of disabilities and very different personalities to begin with, they coped in different ways. When the truck skidded into Trisha's car, she was thrown against the dashboard. Her left hip, right wrist, two fingers of her right hand, and three ribs were broken. She also had a concussion and a deep cut on her forehead. When the ambulance brought her to the hospital emergency room, the doctor put her arm in a cast from fingers to elbow. He stitched the cut and taped her broken ribs. The next day, the surgeon operated on Trisha's hip. Afterward he told her parents, "She has to wear an **abduction brace** for a few months to keep the hip in position, but she should heal well. She should be walking normally in six months to a year."

The shock of the accident was blunted for Trisha by the concussion and the pain medicine. She was groggy for days. By the time her head cleared, she was almost used to lying in a hospital bed with her arm in a cast and her legs tied to a pillow to keep them apart. She was almost used to not being allowed to sit up straight. Besides, her family made it easier for her. Either her mother or father or one of her older sisters was there every afternoon and evening to keep her company and make her comfortable. They combed her hair, helped her into a clean gown, and straightened her bed. They brought her presents and entertained her.

Trisha's parents and sisters were used to taking care of her. They were used to protecting her. So when they told her what the doctors said, they emphasized the good things. They told her that she was lucky that she had only broken bones, that she hadn't damaged any nerves. They assured her that she would get better. But they didn't tell her how long it would take or how hard it would be. Her family didn't realize they were helping Trisha deny how badly hurt she was. They let her believe that she just had to lie in bed for a while before she could get up and walk away.

After a week in bed, when her concussion had healed, Trisha was wheeled to **physical therapy** (or **PT**) on a stretcher. The physical therapist put her on a tilt table and raised her gradually. Trisha complained that she was dizzy, and the therapist lowered her. When she felt better, he raised her again. He was very patient. By the end of the hour, Trisha was able to stay upright without dizziness.

In PT the next day, the therapist brought a wheelchair and showed Trisha how to **transfer** into it without bending her hip all the way. She moaned that she hurt too much to try, but the therapist wasn't so patient this time. He nagged her into doing it. Then he wanted her to wheel the chair. She said her right arm was in a cast. He told her to wheel with her left. That was too much. She cried, "I can't! Leave me alone!"

The therapist said, "I know it's hard. But you have a lot of hard work ahead of you." He described the exercises she would have to do every day and warned her about how carefully she would have to protect her hip until it healed. But Trisha refused to listen. She thought he was just trying to scare her. She was so angry at him for being so mean that she refused to do anything.

That afternoon Trisha complained to her mother about the physical therapist. Her mother said, "He shouldn't have sprung it on you like that, but . . ." Trisha put her hands over her ears. She didn't want to hear about wearing a brace by day and being tied to a pillow at night. She didn't want to know that she couldn't sit up straight or bend over or stand on her left foot for months. She'd been able to bear the misery of the hospital because she believed that everything would be all right soon. Now her mother was telling her that everything was all wrong.

Her mother tried to comfort her. "It's only for a few months." That only upset Trisha more. She couldn't stand months more of this misery. She wanted everything back the way it was before the accident. She buried her head in her pillow and cried and cried.

For Steven, the shock and denial came at the same

time. He simply could not believe that falling off a skateboard could paralyze him. When a fisherman tried to help him, Steven insisted that he was fine, that he would get up in a minute. The man made him lie still while he called 911. Later Steven told the paramedics and emergency room doctors, "I'm okay. I don't feel sick. I just can't move."

The doctors suspected that Steven had a spinal cord injury, and X rays confirmed it. The **spinal cord** carries nerve impulses between the brain and the body, controlling movement and feeling. When the cord is damaged, the muscles below the injury are paralyzed, and feeling is lost in that part of the body. Steven was hurt in the lower back, so he could breathe and use his arms. But he couldn't move or feel his legs.

Further tests showed that he probably had an incomplete lesion, meaning that some of the nerves in his spinal cord were not dead. The doctor told him that he might eventually get some use of his legs back. The doctor said "might eventually"; Steven heard "would soon." The doctor said "some use"; Steven heard "complete cure." Denial often works that way. People hear what they can bear to hear. They distort what was said, or just hear the good parts and tune out the rest.

Denial is not always bad. Steven protected himself against the shock of abruptly becoming paralyzed by believing the paralysis was temporary. That gave him time to gradually get used to being disabled.

Steven was admitted to the hospital and put into a **Stryker frame** to keep him from moving and further damaging his spinal cord. It was like being strapped into a canvas cot with a tight canvas sheet for a blanket. The frame was turned every two hours. Steven stared at the ceiling for two hours and at the floor for the next two. For an active person, it was torture. He kept telling himself, "I'll get out of this thing. I'll get better." When he graduated from the frame to a plastic cast that covered him from armpits to hips, he took it as proof that he was improving. Now he could move his arms. And he'd be able to move his legs as soon as they started working again.

The physical therapist came to Steven's room, massaged his legs, and gave him breathing and arm exercises to do in bed. He was supposed to do sets of ten. He did sets of twenty to get better faster. A few days later, he was wheeled down to PT and put on the tilt table. It seemed stupid to get dizzy when he was only tilted partway up, so when the therapist asked if he felt faint, Steven said, "No."

When he came to, the therapist explained that he'd fainted because the paralysis in his legs affected his circulation. Blood didn't pump back to his brain as well as it did before. Steven promised to tell her if he felt dizzy again. He tuned out the part about the paralysis.

During visiting hours, his parents told him that the bed in the **rehabilitation** center they'd been waiting for would be ready for him next week. Steven didn't remember discussing moving to a **rehab** center (forgetting is one form of denial), but it seemed a step up from the hospital. When his father said he'd make faster progress at the rehab center because it offered the most advanced treatment for long-term patients, Steven screwed up the courage to ask, "How long is long term?"

"Once you're in the rehab center, you'll probably stay for three or four months."

A wave of misery and despair swept over Steven. Then he told himself that he'd work so hard that he'd be out in two months. He could live through two more months

before he walked again. Come to think of it, he'd probably start to walk in the center. Maybe even in a month.
That wouldn't be so bad.

Trisha and Steven were yanked abruptly out of their
everyday lives and confined to hospital beds. Christopher's life was hardly changed by the diagnosis of multiple sclerosis. In fact, once his eye was better and the tests
were over, his life seemed to return to normal.

When the neurologist said he had MS, Christopher
didn't feel shocked. Instead, he was relieved. The diagnosis proved that he was really sick, that it wasn't all in his
mind. He was relieved that his symptoms weren't his
fault, that he hadn't brought them on himself by worrying
about college. And he wasn't frightened, because he
didn't really know what multiple sclerosis is. He wasn't
even sure how to spell it.

The neurologist gave Chris and his mother a booklet
to read. It said that multiple sclerosis is a disease of the
nervous system. The nerves of the brain and spinal cord
are covered with **myelin,** which acts like insulation on
electric wires. In MS, some myelin is destroyed, and the
nerve messages are interrupted. Symptoms range from
occasional blurred vision to blindness, from tingling in an
arm or leg to paralysis. MS usually strikes between the
ages of 15 and 35, but it's hard to predict how it will affect
a particular person. The disease can be mild or severe.
One person becomes paralyzed in a few months; another
goes without symptoms for many years after an attack.
Nobody knows what causes MS, and there is no cure.

After Chris read the booklet, he went to the library. As
a good student, he know how to do research. He
researched MS. He found out that some people have an
acute progressive form of the disease and get steadily

worse. Most people have attacks and remissions. They can be free of symptoms for weeks or months or years. Chris was terrified when he read about the serious cases. He shuddered when he imagined himself in a wheelchair—or worse. Then he read about people who have only a few mild attacks, and he felt better. Why should he be frightened when his symptoms had disappeared? Why should he worry when his eye was fine and he wasn't nearly so tired anymore? He decided that he had a very mild case.

Christopher's denial took a different form from Trisha's and Steven's. Chris didn't deny he had MS. He just denied that it would make a difference in his life. He got upset when his mother worried about his going to college 300 miles away. She reminded him that City College had an excellent engineering program and that he'd been accepted there, too. She said he could easily switch schools.

Chris loved his mother. They were close because it had been just the two of them since his parents' divorce when he was five. But she'd always worried too much about him. And the diagnosis made it worse. He counted himself lucky that his father had offered to pay for any college he chose. Although his father had remarried and moved far away, he was generous with money. So Chris had tried for the best and had been accepted. Now he refused to give up an Ivy League college just because he'd had some trouble with his eye and the doctor put a scary name on it.

The next time his mother mentioned switching to a city college, he blew up. He yelled that he couldn't stand her fussing over him as if he were desperately ill. He accused her of holding on to him because he was all she

had. His mother looked hurt. She said she was only making a suggestion. He said he was going away to college
and that was that. He refused to discuss it anymore.

Chris was sorry he'd hurt his mother's feelings, but he
felt he'd won a victory. Not so much over his mother, but
over multiple sclerosis. It was as if he'd taken on the disease and beaten it.

CHAPTER 2

Starting on the Road Back

I n most illnesses or injuries, there is an acute stage followed by a period of rehabilitation. When you catch the flu, you usually stay in bed for a few days with the acute symptoms: fever, coughing, and weakness. As you begin to feel better, you get up and walk around the house. You go outside for a while and finally return to school. Gradually doing more as you get stronger is a kind of rehabilitation. Rehab can be as short and simple as taking it easy after the flu or as long and difficult as months in a spinal cord injury center after an accident.

The dictionary defines *rehabilitation* (*rehab* for short) as (1) restoring to health or to a former state, (2) fitting patients to take their places in the world again. Whether rehab can restore someone to health or must prepare him or her for a different life-style depends on the particular problem. Although Trisha had many injuries and Steven just one, bones heal and spinal cords rarely do. So Trisha could expect to get better while Steven had to prepare to live without the use of his legs. Trisha's rehabilitation would take months; Steven's would go on in one form or another for the rest of his life.

Rehab begins as soon as possible after an injury. When an accident victim is brought to the hospital, the emergency team goes to work immediately to stop bleeding, ease breathing, set broken bones, and prevent further damage. Once the patient is stable, there is time for tests. A diagnosis is made, and treatment is started. Surgery may be necessary, as in Trisha's case, or the patient may be put in traction, as Steven was. Then rehab starts as soon as possible. The physical therapist was at Steven's bedside when he was released from the Stryker frame, and Trisha went to PT as soon as her concussion healed. They began occupational therapy shortly afterward.

Physical therapy and **occupational therapy** (PT and **OT** for short) are methods of treating the disabilities that result from injury or illness. The goals of both are to help patients recover faster, to improve their physical ability, and to return them to school, work, and play. Although PT and OT overlap in some ways, their emphasis is different. Think of a gym for PT and an arts and crafts class for OT.

PT concentrates on the body. A physical therapist is rather like a sports trainer. In fact, professional athletes turn to physical therapists to prevent injuries as well as to cure them. After an injury, the therapist evaluates the problem and develops an exercise program to build the patient's strength and endurance and to increase flexibility. Exercise can be *passive*, with the therapist moving an affected arm or leg; *assisted*, with the therapist helping the patient move; *active*, with the patient moving himself, or *resistive*, using weights or a machine. Therapists use heat, cold, massage, and/or water therapy to loosen tight muscles and to ease pain, swelling, and muscle **spasms.** Weak or paralyzed muscles may be stimulated electrically.

Physical therapists also teach wheelchair skills and give **gait training** to patients learning how to walk again. If you watch a baby learning to walk, you realize how complicated it is. First the baby balances on both legs. She must keep her balance while she shifts her weight onto one leg and steps forward with the other. Now, shifting her weight onto the forward leg, she lifts her back leg and swings it through and forward. She has taken two steps, but she hasn't mastered flexing her knees, striking with her heel, or rolling her foot—all part of normal adult gait. Keep in mind that the baby's body is working properly.

After an injury a person may need braces, crutches, or a cane for support. The physical therapist supplies them and teaches their use. Did you know that a cane is held in the hand opposite the injured leg and swung forward at the same time as the leg? And think about climbing stairs on crutches.

Wheelchair skills are vital to people whose legs won't support them. Since their arms must do all the work, their exercise program is aimed at strengthening them. And being able to get from wheelchair to bed, bath, or car without help gives people freedom and independence, so they learn transfers. Then there are maneuvers like **wheelies** (jumping a wheelchair up a curb) to master.

While PT works on building strength and getting around, OT addresses **activities of daily living (ADL)**. The things that an able-bodied teen does automatically every day—getting out of bed, washing, dressing, and catching the bus to school—are problems for someone with a disability. How does she put on her socks if she can't bend over? How does he get on the bus in a wheelchair? OT addresses those problems by teaching new ways of doing old tasks and by changing the environment to make the tasks easier.

Occupational therapy uses small-muscle exercises, arts and crafts, and training in tasks ranging from tying shoes to using a computer to teach disabled people to take care of themselves, to function at school or work, and to have fun in their spare time. The therapist suggests or supplies **adaptive equipment** to make life easier. This equipment can be as simple as a "grabber" for out-of-reach things or as high tech as a reading machine that talks. Sometimes an occupational therapist will visit the patient's home or future college dorm to suggest ways of making them more **accessible.**

All medical treatment relies on the patient's cooperation. Antibiotics won't cure an infection if they aren't taken as directed, and a smoker's cough will hang on until he gives up cigarettes. But physical and occupational therapy depend more on the patient than other aspects of medicine. Simply stated: If the patient doesn't work, the therapy doesn't work. We can see the truth of that by looking at how Trisha's and Steven's attitudes about their therapy affected their recoveries.

While Trisha was in the hospital, she went to PT for an hour every day. The first time, she was glad to have a change. After a week in bed, without even being allowed to sit up straight, a ride down the hall on a stretcher was an event. And the PT room looked more like a gym or health club than part of a hospital. There were mats, bars, stacks of weights, stationary bicycles, stairsteppers, and a treadmill.

The physical therapist seemed nice at first. Then he started to push. He didn't seem to understand how much Trisha hurt or how hard everything was for her. He didn't seem to care that she was all bruised from the accident and had only one working arm and leg. He nagged her to do more and more. She moaned that she couldn't, that she hurt too much, that she was too weak, that the concussion made her forget what she learned yesterday. But that didn't stop his pushing or nagging.

First it was the wheelchair. When Trisha complained that it didn't make sense to bother to learn to use one, the physical therapist asked if she planned to lie in bed for the next six months. Then he gave her a lecture on how much strength a person loses for every week in bed. To shut him up, she slid gingerly into the wheelchair. She yelped in pain, louder than she had to, so he would see what he was doing to her. But he just said, "Lean back more," as though he hadn't heard. Then he nagged her to wheel the chair.

Naturally, wheeling one-handed, she went in a circle. She made two circles to show how impossible it was. He showed her how to use the double rim on the wheel to control the chair with her good hand. She said she couldn't. He said, "Try." It was awkward, but it worked. Trisha was surprised at her feeling of accomplishment when she wheeled herself across the room.

But the good feeling didn't last. The next morning she got her brace. She couldn't believe anything could be so uncomfortable. It was like wearing a pair of stiff, hard plastic shorts that covered her from her waist to the middle of her thighs. The brace was made so she couldn't put her legs together or sit up straight or bend over to pick something up. It was horrible. It made her so miserable that she didn't want to move at all. When the aide came to take her to PT, she didn't bother to struggle into her robe.

The therapist said, "Now that you have your brace, we needn't be so careful of your hip. Let's start in the parallel bars. And have your family bring you a sweat suit for tomorrow. Hospital gowns aren't made for walking. Besides, wearing your own clothes will make you feel better."

Trisha muttered, "Nothing'll ever make me feel better." When he said that she might surprise herself, she insisted, "I won't!" She knew she sounded like a cranky baby, but she couldn't help it. That's how she felt. She felt miserable and scared and helpless.

"You're going home soon. If you want to be up on crutches by then, you have to start in the bars now."

A part of Trisha knew he was right. Being stuck in bed was awful, and a wheelchair wasn't much better. She had to learn to use crutches. But she couldn't seem to move. All her life, when something was too hard for her, her mother or father or sisters did it for her. Now, when she was sick and weak, she was on her own. It was too much to bear. She started to cry.

The therapist let her cry it out. Then he handed her a tissue. "Crying helps sometimes. After you dry your eyes, we'll work on exercises for your hand so it won't swell in the cast. By then you'll be ready for the parallel bars."

He wasn't being mean or unsympathetic. He knew that when someone's body is injured, that person's mind and emotions are affected, too. The patient feels frightened and helpless and wants to be taken care of. Even adults who have taken responsibility for their own lives for years may go back to acting childish. For teens, who are closer to childhood, the pull is stronger.

The therapist knew that it was hard for Trisha to work at her rehabilitation, but unless she did, she would not heal properly. So he pushed her for her own good. And she was able to give in to feeling miserable and whining and complaining because she knew he would push her into doing what she had to do. It became a game: Trisha moaned that she couldn't do it, and the therapist made her try.

When she left the hospital, Trisha knew how to use her crutches without putting weight on her left leg. She had a list of exercises to do every day and a gadget from OT for putting on her socks without bending over. A rented wheelchair, a shower bench, and a raised toilet seat were waiting for her at home, along with three new pairs of baggy pants and two full skirts to fit over the brace. It seemed that she was all set.

What she didn't have was a sense of responsibility for her recovery. With her family around to take care of her, she slipped comfortably into the sick-child role. Why should she struggle for ten minutes to put on her socks with the OT gadget when her mother could do it for her in ten seconds? Especially when she was still so weak. Half a block on the crutches wore her out completely. So she didn't go out much. Sometimes her sister took her for an outing in the wheelchair and pushed her, or her father drove her in the car. Mainly she sat in the recliner watching TV or talking on the phone. As for the exercises, she said she'd start them tomorrow.

Without the physical therapist to push her, Trisha sat back, let her family pamper her, and waited to get better. She was shocked when, at a follow-up visit to the doctor, her X rays showed that she wasn't healing as well as expected.

Steven, too, was taking longer than he expected to heal, but not because he wasn't working at getting better. He just didn't realize what having a spinal cord injury meant. He'd broken his collarbone when he was 11, and that had healed perfectly, so why shouldn't he think his spine would do the same? Since he was getting feeling back in his hips, he expected his legs to follow. It just seemed to be taking an awfully long time.

When he told the doctor he could feel his hips, the doctor said, "Good. That means that you'll have use of your hip muscles. We expected that because the injury is rather low in your back, but one can never be sure. Hip muscles are important for good balance in a wheelchair. And if hip control is good enough, there is the possibility of walking with long braces."

Steven was so happy to hear the magic word "walking" that he didn't pay attention to the rest. He figured that the harder he worked, the sooner he would walk again. So he went at his physical therapy as if he were training for the Olympics. Because he was still getting dizzy on the tilt table, he practiced the breathing exercises the physical therapist said would help. He blew into the gadget she'd given him until he had no breath left. He lay patiently under hot packs to relax the spasms in his paralyzed leg muscles and endured electrical stimulation to make them contract properly. He faithfully did the exercises to strengthen his trunk, shoulders, and arms in preparation for using a wheelchair.

He'd hoped to be in a wheelchair before he was transferred to the rehab center, but he couldn't overcome the dizziness in time. He left the hospital the same way he'd come in, on a wheeled stretcher in an ambulance. Lying strapped on the stretcher, he promised himself to work even harder at the rehab center.

CHAPTER 3

The Next Steps

There are many rehabilitation services for people who are sick, injured, or disabled. Not just physical therapy and occupational therapy, but psychotherapy, vocational counseling, support groups, social services, recreational and educational programs. Doctors, nurses, **psychologists**, **social workers**, PT and OT therapists, group leaders, and teachers can help in the rehab process. But which services, if any, someone receives depends on what is wrong with him— and where he is.

You are more likely to get at least some rehabilitation if you are injured than if you are ill. Doctors prescribe rehab more often in the hospital than in their offices because most hospitals have rehab departments. Big-city hospitals usually offer more services than small local ones, and specialized rehab centers have the most complete programs. You will probably get an hour a day of rehab in a general hospital and a full day in a rehab center. If you are not hospitalized, you have a better chance of getting help if you know what is available and ask for it. And you are more apt to know if you belong to an organization for people with your condition.

Steven and Trisha were both injured and hospitalized.

It was routine for their doctors to prescribe PT for them. It was also common practice for a hospital social worker to meet with them and their parents to see what other help they needed. After consulting with the doctor, the social worker spoke to Steven's parents about the advantages of transferring him to a rehab center. Then she helped them find a good center. Before Trisha left the hospital, the social worker made sure there was someone to help her at home and arranged for the equipment she needed.

Trisha's doctor examined her before she went home and made an appointment to see her in six weeks. Since she couldn't start any new exercises until her hip healed, he didn't prescribe more PT. He just told her to continue her exercise program on her own. Trisha's rehab was now her responsibility. If she didn't take the responsibility and her family let her evade it, there was nobody to tell them they were making a mistake. They were on their own now.

Christopher and his mother were on their own after his MS was diagnosed. The neurologist said that since the symptoms had cleared up, he preferred not to start Chris on medication. If Chris had another attack, he would put him on cortisone for a short while. The doctor gave Chris a booklet to read and told him just to go on with his life and to call if he had another attack.

Doctors concentrate on diagnosing and treating diseases. They rarely have the time or training to help patients cope with the practical and emotional problems the diseases cause. If Chris had been in the hospital, he probably would have seen a social worker, and his doctor might have asked the hospital psychologist to talk with him. But in the doctor's office he just got a diagnosis, a short explanation, and a booklet.

The booklet described MS and listed the possible symptoms. It didn't tell Chris how the disease would affect his life. There was nobody to ask, and when he read up on the subject, he couldn't find any cases that sounded like his. They all seemed to involve people who were a lot sicker than he was. So he followed the doctor's advice to go on with his life. He started getting ready to go away to college. He tried to decide whether to get a summer job or to take advanced math in summer school and get a head start on his college studies.

His mother read about MS, too, and what she read worried her. She worried about Chris going away to college. What if he had an attack at school? Would he have good medical care? Would there be someone to take care of him? Why wouldn't he switch to a city college and live at home so she could be sure he was all right?

Although she'd agreed to his going away before he got sick, she felt that the situation had changed. She didn't understand how much he wanted to be on his own. She thought he was being foolish and stubborn. Chris told her there was a health clinic at school. He said he wasn't going to have another attack, but if he did, the clinic doctor would give him some cortisone. He didn't understand why his mother was so worried. He thought she was being foolish and overprotective.

Months later, Christopher's mother would hear about the MS Society. She would attend the meetings for families of people with the disease, share her worries with the group, and find out how other people coped. But right after the diagnosis, she and Chris were on their own. So they argued about college. Chris was angry at his mother's trying to break her promise, and she was hurt that he didn't know she was doing it for his good. There was nobody to tell them that people often find something to be hurt and angry about as a way of not facing other painful feelings.

Finally, his mother agreed that Chris could go away to college—if he didn't have another attack. For a while he felt that he'd regained control of his life. Then he caught a virus—a mild virus. Just a sore throat and some dizziness and fever. The fever was gone in a day and his throat felt better, but he remained strangely off balance. He figured that the virus was hanging on and took some vitamin C. He didn't mention it to his mother because she was such a worrier.

Then he fell walking across the living room. He was carrying an armful of library books to his bedroom. He wasn't thinking about walking; he expected his body to work without his paying attention. But it surprised him by tipping to the side. He stumbled and pitched forward. The books went flying.

He wasn't hurt, just puzzled. He looked to see what he'd tripped over, but he couldn't find anything. He laughed it off when his mother came running to see what happened. Picking up his books, he started toward his room. His mother asked, "What's wrong with your leg? Why are you limping?"

It wasn't a bad attack: just the off-balance feeling and some numbness on one side of his body. The cortisone cleared it up in a week. But the attack left Chris frightened and unsure. He told the doctor the symptoms were completely gone, but he wasn't positive they were. Was he still a little off balance, or was he imagining it? Would he have another attack soon? A bad one? He didn't protest when his mother asked the doctor if it would be better for him to go to college nearby. The doctor said it

might be a good idea—at least until they saw how the disease developed.

Filling out the form to change colleges was like writing
in black and white that he was a sick person. It exhausted
him. Fatigue is a symptom of MS, and the doctor had told
Chris to be sure he got enough rest. So he didn't register
for summer school or look for a summer job. He spent a
lot of time sitting in his room, hardly seeing anyone—not
even his best friend. He was too tired. But hanging around
his room just made him more tired and depressed. His
mother worried about him, but she didn't know what to
do. And she had nowhere to turn for advice.

Trisha, Christopher, and Steven lived in a large city
where excellent medical care was available. Trisha's surgeon was a specialist in rebuilding shattered hips. Christopher's neurologist used **magnetic resonance imaging
(MRI)** to give him a quick diagnosis that saved months of
uncertainty. But when it came to rehabilitation, Chris got
no help at all, and Trisha's stopped when she left the hospital. Only Steven got all the rehab he needed.

Steven spent a month in a general hospital before
being transferred to a spinal cord injury unit in a rehab
center. He expected it to be like the hospital with more PT.
Hospital life is mostly lying in bed waiting. He had waited
for the nurse to wash and change him in the morning, for
the aide to bring his breakfast, for the doctor to examine
him. He killed time listening to his radio or talking to his
current roommate while he waited for someone to take
him down to PT, for his lunch to come, for visiting hours
to start. Then he waited for the sleeping pill to knock him
out for the night.

His first day in the rehab center was totally different.
The morning nurse didn't just rush in, get him set for the

day, and hurry out. She asked him how far he could sit up and for how long. Could he get back up if he bent over? Steven didn't know. He hadn't thought about things like that, only about walking again. The nurse made him try every part of his morning routine himself before she helped him. It was surprising how much he could do. He was sorry when she left.

He picked at his breakfast, listening to his radio and wishing he had a roommate to talk to. But he wasn't alone for long. People came in one after another to examine him. They moved his arms and legs around and tapped him with rubber hammers and pricked him with pins. They asked him lots of questions. Although they all introduced themselves, Steven couldn't keep track of who was who. The man who questioned him about the tilt table had to be the physical therapist, and the woman who asked how he felt about being in a rehab center was the psychologist—or was she the social worker? By evening, he was exhausted. He fell asleep without a pill.

They tested him the next day. They took his blood and X-rayed him and put him in a machine that belonged on *Star Trek*. The following morning a doctor came to talk to him. She said she was the **physiatrist**; her field was rehabilitation medicine. The people who had examined Steven worked together as a team, and she was the team coordinator. The physiatrist gave Steven his schedule. He had PT and OT for an hour every morning, beginning today. Regular school didn't start for another two weeks, but SCI classes were three times a week. His first class was this afternoon. He'd see the psychologist twice a week, and a social worker had arranged an appointment with his parents. Recreation therapy and vocational counseling could wait a while, but the weekly group meeting was important. And, of course, he'd want to join in some of the evening and weekend activities.

As soon as the doctor left, Steven was wheeled to PT, where the therapist started him on sitting balance. The therapist said Steven was lucky that his hip muscles worked. Although the muscles were weak from not being used, he'd be sitting in a wheelchair in no time. Steven thought he'd be luckier if his leg muscles worked, but he concentrated on not passing out or tipping over.

The occupational therapist measured him for a wheelchair. Steven hadn't known they came in different sizes and weights, that the arms could be fixed or detachable, or that there were different kinds of arms, tires, rims, footrests, and brakes. The therapist said she'd look through the center's wheelchairs for a lightweight one with detachable arms for him. She warned him not to buy his own until he'd used a wheelchair for a while and knew what features he wanted. The way she talked about his buying a wheelchair bothered him. Was it going to take longer to walk again than he'd thought?

Lunch was next. After a morning of PT and OT, Steven was hungry enough to eat it. Then came SCI class. The nurse who taught it used a chart to show that the higher up on the spine the injury was, the more paralysis resulted. **Quadriplegics' (quads)** injuries were in the neck or upper spine, so their arms were at least partly paralyzed. **Paraplegics' (paras)** injuries were in the lower back, so the paralysis started below the waist. Steven was a para. The nurse told them that a spinal cord injury affected everything the body did. In the next classes she would explain how breathing, movement, digestion, elimination, circulation, and the skin worked before and after the injury. She would teach them how to take care of every part of their bodies. She promised that they'd end up knowing as much about spinal cord injury and self-care as she did.

It was hard for Steven to concentrate on what she was saying because it was the first time he'd seen other people with spinal cord injuries. There were six other people in the class. Two were on wheeled stretchers like his; four were in wheelchairs. There was only one female, and everyone seemed to be under 30. Without staring, Steven couldn't tell who was a quad and who was a para like him. He kept wanting to stare and at the same time not to look.

Later he tried to explain to the psychologist how he felt. "It was like they made it real for me. Like looking in a mirror and seeing myself. That really threw me, and I wanted to get away from them."

It is not easy to get away when you can't walk or use a wheelchair. Waiting to be taken to his room, Steven's stretcher was parked next to another one. The guy on it told him there was a *Rocky* movie in the lounge tonight. Steven said he was too knocked out.

Later, someone from the SCI class came into Steven's room in a wheelchair. He introduced himself as Aaron, and they talked about how nice the nurses were and how awful the food was. As Aaron left, he said, "It all takes some getting used to, but don't hide too long." When Steven said he wasn't hiding, Aaron answered, "Good. A belly dancer's coming Friday night. You don't want to miss that. And I'll see you at the group meeting tomorrow."

Steven was thrown together with the other patients in SCI classes, group meetings, pool exercises, OT projects, community dining nights, and weekend recreation. When he got his wheelchair, he met them in the TV room and the lounge. He soon stopped trying to avoid them. Being among guys whose bodies didn't work either, who were struggling with the same problems he was, made him feel less like a freak. It helped him to stop denying what had happened to him. In many ways, the other patients were as important to his rehabilitation as the doctors, nurses, and therapists.

Aaron, the center daredevil, became Steven's special friend, but he became close to the others, too. It was as though they were on the same team, trying to pull themselves out of the basement and win the pennant. The other guys were there to egg him on when he tried something new or to joke him out of it when he was down. They shared experiences and gave him tips. After watching Aaron do wheelies, Steven was able to pop one the first time he tried in PT. And he found that he could talk to the others more easily than to his family when they visited. Only people who'd been through it could understand what it was like for him.

During his months at the rehabilitation center, Steven learned new ways of doing things he had once taken for granted. He strengthened his body and became good at the special care it needed. He mastered wheelchair skills. He became as independent as possible. Although he didn't give up hope that the twitching and tingling in his legs meant he'd eventually be able to use them again, he gradually came to terms with his disability.

Steven wasn't the only one who had to learn to cope with his disability. His disability changed his whole family's lives. The center held weekly meetings for patients' families, where Steven's parents and brother learned many of the same things Steven learned in SCI class. The team members involved in Steven's rehab also helped his family. The physical therapist taught them about wheel-chair transfers and how to get the chair up a curb. The psychologist helped them to deal with their grief and fears; she also advised them how to help Steven deal with his. Before Steven left the rehab center, the occupational therapist went to his home to suggest ways to make it wheelchair-accessible. The social worker helped his parents plan for his return.

Four months after Steven fell off his skateboard—one month spent in the hospital and three in the rehab center—he went home. He was ready to pick up his life again, and his family was ready to help him.

CHAPTER 4

Picking Up Life Again

The months after an accident or the onset of a serious disease can be divided into three stages. There is the acute stage: being hospitalized or ill at home. Ordinary life is put on hold while the patient copes with the symptoms, with the loss of freedom, and with uncertainty about the future. Next comes the rehabilitation stage: working to regain health and strength or learning new ways of living. Rehab can mean months in a SCI center, weeks of PT in a hospital or as an outpatient, or struggling on one's own to adjust to the condition. Whether people have doctors and therapists or just their families to help with their rehab, eventually they move into the third stage: picking up life again. They return to normal living—even if what is normal for them has changed drastically.

Ideally, they start adjusting to the injury or disease while it is being treated, use the rehabilitation stage to learn to cope with any resulting disability, and then return to normal life better able to deal with the remaining problems. Unfortunately, it doesn't always work that way.

Trisha seemed to make a fairly good adjustment to her injury in the hospital. She was childish and whiny, but that is normal for someone who is only 14, hurts all over, and has her ribs taped, her right arm in a cast, and half her body in a brace. Her hospital rehab also went fairly well. True, the physical therapist had to push her, but Trisha mastered the wheelchair and crutches and learned her exercises. And not doing anything when she first got home was understandable because she was still weak, stiff, and achy. A week or two of skipping exercises just meant she would have to work harder at them later.

The problem was that one or two weeks stretched into six. Because Trisha felt weak and clumsy and sorry for herself, she sat in the recliner all day. Her family dressed her and served her meals and brought her whatever she wanted. They did everything for her—except, of course, her exercises. But as any physical therapist will tell you: Use it or lose it. Behaving as if she were glued to the recliner kept Trisha weak and made her stiffer and achier. Which made her even sorrier for herself and less likely to do anything. Going to school might have broken the cycle, but she had **home instruction** until her hip healed. The teacher came for two hours in the morning, and Trisha spent a little while doing her homework on the computer with her left hand. The rest of the time she sat watching TV.

When the doctor examined her after she was home six weeks, he read her the riot act. He said he'd done his job, and the physical therapist had done his, but Trisha wasn't doing hers. Her leg muscles had shortened, and she'd lost some range of motion in her knee and hip joints. He asked her if she wanted to be a cripple for the rest of her life. Then he told her mother to stop coddling Trisha and to see that she did a full hour of exercises every day. An hour in the morning and another hour in the evening would be even better. He said he expected an enormous improvement the next time he saw them. When Trisha's mother told the rest of the family what the doctor said, everyone had a suggestion. Her father suggested, "Walking with crutches is good exercise. Trisha should get out more." One sister said, "She should dress herself." The other sister said, "I'll bet she could set the table at night."

Nobody asked Trisha what she thought or felt. It didn't occur to them that the doctor might have frightened her into making up her mind to start exercising tomorrow. Or that she was bored with hanging around the house and planned to get out and visit her friend Beth tomorrow. They acted as if it was all her fault she wasn't healing right, and it was up to them to get her well. They made her so mad that she hobbled to her bedroom and slammed the door.

She stayed mad as she dressed herself and walked with her crutches and exercised. She was mad at how hard it was to do everything. It took forever to get washed and dressed in the morning with the brace and cast in the way. She wanted to rip the stupid things off and throw them out the window. She wanted to toss the crutches after them. And the exercises were torture. Her mother made her exercise twice a day while one of her sisters watched to see that she didn't cheat. She did the exercises, but she sulked and complained and "accidentally" knocked over a lamp with her cast.

Trisha was angry at her family and blamed them for her misery. She had some justice on her side. First they had taken over and coddled her; then they stood over her to make her take care of herself. It was reasonable to resent being treated like a baby. But she was also using her family as targets for the frustration and misery of not having gotten better automatically. If she blamed them, she didn't have to blame herself for not having done anything for six weeks.

The doctor was pleased the next time he examined Trisha. Her muscles were stronger, and her joints moved more freely. He said if she kept up the good work, she should be able to put weight on her leg by the time the cast came off her arm next month. Then she could start PT again. Trisha's mother said that was wonderful. Trisha didn't say anything. PT would just be one more thing for her family to hound her about. Her mother sighed. It bothered her that Trisha was so angry and difficult lately, but she told herself that the important thing was that Trisha was getting better. She would be healed in a few more months, and then she'd be her old cheerful self again. Trisha's mother tried to be patient until life returned to normal.

She was right to be patient. **Regression,** acting babyish or difficult, is a common reaction to a serious injury or illness. When Trisha came home from the hospital, she went through a period of being dependent and self-indulgent. Now she was sulky and angry. But she was doing what she had to do. As long as she continued to follow the doctor's orders, she would eventually get well. She would follow the pattern of hospital care, rehabilitation, and return to normal living.

Christopher's pattern was different. He wasn't hospitalized, and it was months before he had any rehab. Because there was no way to know how serious a case of multiple sclerosis he had, he couldn't predict what normal living would be for him. He had to wait and see.

Chris spent the months after the diagnosis feeling like

a Ping-Pong ball. He bounced back and forth between denial and despair, between believing he would never have another attack and worrying that he'd end up in a wheelchair or, worse still, blind. One minute he blamed his mother for making him switch to a city college; the next minute he was glad not to be hundreds of miles away from her in case he got sick again.

He really liked college, although the work was hard and he was often tired. His mother wanted him to tell his professors he had MS so he could get extra time for assignments. Chris refused. He refused to tell anyone. When his old friends had asked why he'd changed his mind about going away to school, he'd said it was too expensive. And he certainly didn't want his new class-mates to know there was anything wrong with him. When he was tired, Chris told them he'd stayed up all night studying. When he was sick, he said he had a virus. Since he didn't have crutches like Trisha or a wheelchair like Steven to announce his condition, he could pretend he was healthy. Sometimes he convinced himself that he really was healthy. Other times he felt as though he was living a lie. And sometimes he longed for someone to talk to.

Christopher had two very different reactions when his mother joined the local chapter of the MS Society. He wouldn't go to meetings with her, but he listened eagerly when she told him what she had learned. He was both frightened and hopeful when she arranged for him to get a second opinion at a clinic that specialized in treat-ing MS.

The clinic used the same team approach to multiple sclerosis that Steven's rehab center used with spinal cord injuries. (In fact, the MS clinic and the SCI unit were both part of the same large hospital complex.) Chris was examined by a neurologist, a psychologist, and a physical therapist. Although the team agreed with the first neurologist not to put Chris on medication, they felt that something *could* be done for him. They started him on an exercise program to improve his balance and build his muscle strength and a diet to keep him healthy and raise his energy level. They put his name down for a support group for teens that was scheduled to begin soon. Seven months after he was first told he had MS, Chris's rehabilitation began.

About the time that Christopher was starting rehab, Steven left the rehab center to begin the next stage of his recovery: going home. Although he would return to the center later for physical therapy as an outpatient, the time had come for him to pick up his life again. That meant facing how different life would be from now on.

The rehab team tried to make Steven's transition from the center to home easier. Toward the end of his stay, Steven had self-care days when he did everything for himself, practicing for the time there wouldn't be a nurse nearby. And he had already been out on passes with his parents. The first time, they just spent an hour in the park and bought ice-cream cones. The next time, his brother Paul came along, and they all watched a sandlot baseball game and went to a pizzeria. On the last Saturday before he was discharged, Steven left the center at nine in the morning and didn't return until bedtime. So he was surprised at how nervous he was about going home for good.

His house was on two floors. While Steven was away, his father and brother, with his uncle who was a carpenter, made the first floor wheelchair accessible. They built a ramp up the porch stairs. They converted the downstairs den into a bedroom for him. They widened the door to the downstairs bathroom and installed grab bars and a hand-held shower. His mother moved snack foods and dishes to the lower kitchen cabinets so Steven could help himself when he was hungry. And she took a month off from work so she could be with him until he "settled in."

His family did everything possible to make Steven's return home easy. They put the extra TV in his new room along with his tape player and cassettes. They even moved the posters he had had on his bedroom walls. All his posters, including the one his brother had claimed was his, were there. When Steven saw the posters, he had to blow his nose hard. They'd gone to so much trouble for him, but it just reminded him that he couldn't go upstairs anymore. It pointed out how much he had changed, how different he was from them now. In the rehab center everyone was like him. Now that he was back home, he felt like a cripple.

It bothered him that his parents and brother stood up when they talked to him. Before his accident, Steven had been 6'2". He was used to looking down to talk to people. Now, sitting in his wheelchair, he was only 3'6". If his family stood up, he had the choice of staring at their chests or craning his neck to see their faces. But he was ashamed to ask them to sit down.

Although it didn't make sense, he was ashamed of a lot of things, including how long it took him to do everything. He'd learned to shower, go to the bathroom, and dress himself at the rehab center. He could transfer in and out of his wheelchair. He could get up curbs and into cars. He knew how to use a bus lift and what to ask when he called a movie or restaurant. The social worker had said he was ready for "independent living," but she didn't warn him how long the simple routines of life would take. Before the accident, he could be out of bed and onto the bus to school in three-quarters of an hour, less if he skipped breakfast. Now it took him almost two hours to get ready in the morning.

Steven was also ashamed when people—even his family—saw him struggling to do something. It made him angry when they helped him without asking. It even bothered him when he'd asked for help because he felt that he should be able to do everything easily by himself.

He felt his face get red when people in the street looked at his wheelchair and quickly looked away as if it was his fault he couldn't walk. Maybe it was. If he hadn't been going so fast on his skateboard or if he'd looked where he was going. . . . The way people looked at him made him uncomfortable about going out.

Besides, going places was such a hassle. Everything had to be planned in advance. No more running out for burgers with the guys when they got hungry at ten at night. Not only did he have to make sure somebody had a car so he could get to the diner and then go through the hassle of getting himself and his wheelchair in and out of the car, but he also had to worry about getting inside once they got there. He had to call ahead and ask if the diner was wheelchair accessible. Then the person who answered the phone wouldn't know, so he'd have to ask for the manager. Even after the manager said "yes," there was a chance he'd get there and find he had to go in the back door and through the kitchen. The burger wasn't worth making a fool of himself in front of the other guys. Even if everything worked out, it wasn't worth all the planning. He would rather stay home by himself.

There were plenty of frustrations at home, too, such as having to jump to reach light switches. Or trying to maneuver his wheelchair on the living room rug. (It was like riding a bike in soft sand.) Or having to wheel out the front door, down the ramp, and all the way around the house to the garage when it was two steps from the back door. But the frustrations at home weren't as bad as wheeling down the block to see an old friend and not realizing he couldn't get up the porch steps until they loomed in front of him. Or what happened when he went to his grandmother's for Sunday dinner.

His parents had planned the visit well. They went by car, and there was a baby carriage ramp down to the basement and an elevator up to the apartment. His grandmother had removed a dining room chair so Steven could wheel up to the table. Even talking to his relatives wasn't so bad because they were all sitting down. The trouble came when they had coffee in the living room. Steven had parked next to a little end table so he could put his coffee cup down. Suddenly he had a leg spasm. His leg kicked out and knocked over the end table. The coffee poured all over his grandmother's prized Oriental rug.

It wasn't just ruining his grandmother's rug that made him not want to go anywhere anymore. It wasn't just having to plan everything or finding that places weren't wheelchair accessible that made him withdraw. It was all the big and little frustrations put together. In the rehab center, each thing he learned to do for himself was a victory. Each skill he mastered seemed to bring him a step nearer to returning to his old life. But being at home made it clear that he wasn't going back to his old life. Everything he did and every place he went pointed out the difference between the way it was then and the way it was now.

The contrast between what he could do and what he wanted to do was too much for him to bear. The depression that he'd fought off during the months in the hospital and rehab center finally caught up with him. Nobody can absorb the blow of a major injury and go on being brave and hardworking forever. Steven had done it for longer than most people. Now, like Trisha, he had to regress for a while. At least temporarily, he gave up the fight and withdrew into himself.

CHAPTER 5

Being Disabled

There were many reasons for Steven's depression, such as the everyday practical problems and his loss of freedom. It was discouraging to have to struggle to do what other people did so easily. It was miserable not to be able to go where he wanted when he wanted. He hated having to plan every little thing. But his depression was also caused by the same thing that made Christopher refuse to tell anyone he had multiple sclerosis: loss of self-esteem.

Both Steven and Chris felt less valuable than they were before the injury and illness. Like most of the 40 million Americans who have disabilities, they were not born disabled. Since they had been "normal" all their lives, they carried the same pictures of "the disabled" in their minds that most able-bodied people do. Now they had a hard time fitting themselves into those pictures.

A 1991 Harris Poll was the first large national study of our society's feelings about people with disabilities. It showed that almost all able-bodied American adults admired disabled people but that pity went along with the admiration. Most of those interviewed said, "I pity the disabled for the awful burdens they have to bear and admire them for keeping going. I'm not sure I could do it."

The interviewees believed that there is discrimination against disabled people. They supported laws to make it easier for the disabled to work, travel, and take active roles in society. However, the majority of people questioned were uncomfortable around someone with a disability. This reaction was true of half of those who had a disabled friend or relative, while three-quarters of those who did not know anyone who had a disability felt awkward or embarrassed when they met someone who did. In other words, they reacted to the disability rather than to the person who had it. They felt that disabled people were different, and they didn't know how to treat them.

Is it surprising that Steven didn't want to go out in his wheelchair or that Christopher hid his illness? Not only was it hard for them to face the attitudes of the people around them, but they also carried the same attitudes in their own heads. They felt embarrassed and ashamed of themselves. Trisha was spared these feelings because she knew that her cast, brace, and crutches were temporary.

According to the poll, the public sees the disabled as a group of people who are different, admirable, and pitiful. Too often this attitude is supported by the media. If you go to the movies, watch TV, or read most books, you are likely to come away feeling that all disabled people are either the helpless victims shown on the telethons or the superheroes of the movies of the week.

Although telethons raise a lot of money for the research and treatment of disabling diseases, they play on viewers' sympathy to get them to open their wallets. Telethons stress the horror of the disease and show the worst cases. People who have the disease are presented as pitiful—although usually cute, cheerful, or courageous—victims who are dependent on the viewers' charity. Since they are rarely shown leading ordinary lives, viewers get the impression that few people with chronic diseases or disabilities are capable of doing so. Many disabled people, particularly those in the disability rights movement, believe that telethons do more harm than good because they present false images.

Movies and TV shows often present an opposite but equally false image: stories of superhuman struggle and courage in which a sick or disabled person overcomes all obstacles to achieve a special goal. Or else the shows are about a person who can't adjust to his or her disability and is bitter or self-pitying. (The self-pitier is usually female, and the bitter person is usually male.) Finally a friend, lover, or family member shocks the disabled person into becoming strong and brave and mastering her or his problems.

These stories may be dramatic, but they do not reflect reality. In real life most disabled people neither climb mountains nor hide in closets. They are ordinary people trying to lead ordinary lives. They are people like Christopher and Steven and Trisha—people like you and me.

When the Harris Poll asked people how they felt about the disabled, they didn't ask them what they meant by "disabled." But from the answers to the other questions, it seems that the interviewees carried pictures in their minds of severe visible disabilities like Steven's. A wheelchair, a white cane, or the jerky movements of cerebral palsy told them that someone was disabled, and they felt uncomfortable with that person. Since most able-bodied people don't get to know disabled people as individuals, they tend to lump them into a single group. They don't realize that disabled people are as different from one another as nondisabled people are. They often take the disabled part for the whole person. Without thinking it through, they assume that someone who is disabled in one way is disabled in every way. They raise their voices when speaking to someone who is blind or ask a wheelchair user's friend what the person in the chair wants to eat.

These attitudes usually don't extend to disabilities and chronic illnesses that don't advertise themselves. So people with hidden disabilities, like a hearing loss or a disease like Christopher's that flares up from time to time, are tempted to "pass for normal" in order to be accepted. They would rather be thought lazy when they are sick or stuck-up when they don't hear than be lumped with "the disabled."

This is a good place to ask exactly what a disability is. The dictionary defines disability as "A condition that lasts for at least six months and interferes with performing some activities of living." That is a good definition, but it doesn't answer several important questions. How much does the disability interfere? With what activities? Can the person with the disability compensate for it? Could he or she be helped to compensate?

Juan seems disabled when you look at his left hand. He was born with only a thumb on that hand. But he skillfully uses the fingers on his other hand to make up for the missing ones. He is studying computers, and his six fingers are as quick on the keyboard as other people's ten. Is he really disabled?

Now think about Steven wanting to see a friend. Steven can't walk or climb stairs. His disability stops him from visiting his friend because he can't get up the porch stairs. But what if the friend's house had a ramp instead of stairs?

A disability doesn't always have to be a handicap. Although in the past the words *disability* and **handicap** were used to mean the same thing, handicap now refers to the barrier or situation that keeps a disabled person from doing something. The stairs are a handicap to Steven. His disability would not stop him from visiting his friends if there were a ramp.

Many disabled people are not handicapped when they use adaptive equipment. Gaylord wears glasses to see the board in class. Because so many people wear glasses, they aren't considered disabled or seen as using adaptive equipment. And as long as Gaylord doesn't break his glasses, he isn't handicapped. He does his schoolwork as if he had perfect vision. Now compare him to Yoko, who is blind. She has a guide dog to lead her into class. She uses a Braille textbook and takes notes on a tape recorder. It takes more adaptive equipment to keep Yoko from being handicapped in class, but is she so different from Gaylord?

People are often labeled "disabled" or "normal," but the difference between them is not as great as it seems at first glance. All people—whether they are healthy or sick, able-bodied or disabled in some way—have abilities as well as disabilities. Everyone does some things well and some with difficulty and has some things he or she can't do at all. Some "normal" people become Olympic athletes; others get winded running half a block. Some people play the piano, guitar, and flute; others can't carry a tune. Some can do long division in their heads; others can't figure out how much to leave for a tip in a restaurant. Christopher tires easily, but he aces his math and science tests. Steven can't walk, but he never refuses a challenge. Trisha wears a cast and brace, but she has a good sense of humor. Every person is different, and everyone wants to be accepted for who he or she is.

Although the Harris Poll showed that this acceptance hasn't come yet, it also suggests that attitudes toward the disabled are changing. Half of the people polled who had a disabled relative or friend did feel at ease with other disabled people. The key here is familiarity. When they got to know them, the interviewees found that the seemingly different people who limped or shook or stuttered were just Steven and Chris and Trisha.

Even those who were embarrassed by not knowing how to treat disabled people supported their civil rights. An overwhelming 98 percent of all the people polled believed that every American—including people with disabilities—deserved an equal opportunity to take part in society. They supported laws to make changes in the workplace so that qualified disabled people could hold jobs. They also backed laws making transportation and public places like restaurants and stores accessible to everyone. Perhaps most important, they believed that laws to help people with disabilities are good for the country as a whole.

This belief that disabled people can contribute to society is a fairly new one. In the past, the disabled were seen as burdens to be cared for by their families and kept out of the way. Today people with disabilities are students, teachers, carpenters, computer programmers, office managers, engineers, doctors, and lawyers. They grow crops or raise children. They run marathons or run for public office. Today more disabled people are taking an active part in society than at any other time in history, and still more are joining the mainstream every day.

This change did not occur quickly or easily. It has

taken almost 50 years, and many factors have helped bring it about. One factor is the larger number of disabled people today because modern medicine keeps people alive who would have died in the past. Before insulin, diabetes was a killer disease. Today most diabetics live productive lives, but they have a higher risk of being disabled by blindness or amputation than the rest of the population. A soldier whose spinal cord was injured in World War I (1914-1918) usually died within a few weeks. But so many soldiers and civilians survived spinal cord injuries and amputations during World War II (1939-1945) that the new specialty of rehabilitation medicine was developed to care for them. And many paralyzed veterans of World War II are still alive. Today people like Steven can expect to lead full and active lives.

Diabetes and spinal cord injuries are only two of the many disabilities that modern medicine can treat but not cure. As a result, there is a large minority today—about 17 percent of all Americans—who have some kind of disability. Like other minorities, they have demanded equal rights. During the Civil Rights movement of the 1950s and 1960s, disabled people protested, demonstrated, and called for laws to bring them into the mainstream of American society.

The first of these laws was the Federal Rehabilitation Act of 1973. This stopped corporations that did business with the federal government from discriminating against people with disabilities. Because of this law, thousands of disabled people got jobs and/or promotions and were able to support themselves. It also opened colleges to disabled students. The Education for All Handicapped Children Act came a year later. This guaranteed all elementary and high-school students with disabilities a proper education. Under this law, many disabled children went to school for the first time. Many others were **mainstreamed**. They were taken out of special classes and mixed with able-bodied students.

The most recent and most sweeping law is the Americans with Disabilities Act of 1990 (ADA). The ADA guarantees equal job opportunity and equal access to transportation, telephone service, and public places. The earlier laws opened schools and jobs in large corporations to disabled people; the ADA forbids job discrimination in small companies as well. It also requires changes in buses, trains, airports, hotels, theaters, sports arenas, restaurants, parks, zoos, museums, libraries, gymnasiums, shopping centers, stores, banks, hospitals, and doctors' and lawyers' offices so disabled people can use all of them.

The ADA will take several years to go fully into effect and it has some exceptions. Companies having fewer than 25 workers are not covered. Public places only have to make "readily achievable" changes or provide "alternative methods." In other words, the Metropolitan Museum of Art doesn't have to build a ramp on the long flight of marble steps leading to the front entrance because a wheelchair user can go through the side entrance to the elevator. And if Steven's school is not wheelchair accessible, the Board of Education can transfer him to a school that is.

The ADA is not perfect, and it will take time—and probably some lawsuits—to effect all the necessary changes. But the law will help to get Steven out of the house. He'll be able to take the bus to the mall and buy himself a T-shirt and some new tapes. He'll go to a basketball game and have a snack afterward without worrying if he can get into the stadium or restaurant. He can take a trip to Disneyland with his family and know that he won't be shut out of the fun.

The ADA should also help him feel better about himself by changing the way other people feel about him. The public's acceptance of people with disabilities has been slowly growing since the rehabilitation and education acts of the 1970s. As able-bodied and disabled people went to school together or worked together, they stopped seeing one another as "different." Now, as the ADA removes the physical barriers, more disabled people will mingle with the able-bodied in stores and buses and theaters. They will become an ordinary part of the crowd. Steven's wheelchair will stop drawing curious stares. And as other people feel more comfortable with him, Steven should feel more comfortable with himself.

Laws can change what people do and indirectly change how they feel. The media can change feelings directly. Movies and TV mirror the public's attitudes, but they also help to shape attitudes. In the past few years there has been a change in the media's images of the disabled. An occasional movie or TV program now focuses on a disabled person's abilities. Some commercials now show a disabled person using the advertiser's product. Advertisers feel that the ADA will bring more disabled shoppers into the stores, and the stores want the business.

The purpose of the ADA is to guarantee equal rights for all, the aim of the movies is to entertain, and the aim of the commercials is to make money. But they are also helping to educate the public. Hopefully, when a future poll asks "Are you uncomfortable with someone who is disabled?" the answer will be, "Of course not."

CHAPTER 6

Support Groups

A serious injury or a chronic disease hurts more than the body. Whether a disability is temporary, permanent, or intermittent, it affects everyday activities and plans for the future. Because it interferes with school, work, fun, friends, and family life, it changes a person's picture of who he is and what he can do. So a rehabilitation program should address the mind as well as the body, feelings as well as practical problems.

Steven saw the psychologist twice a week during his months at the rehab center. He'd always thought only crazy people went to a psychologist or psychiatrist, so he spent the first session trying to prove he wasn't crazy. He insisted that he felt fine, that his accident hadn't gotten him down. Finally the psychologist smiled and said, "If losing the use of your legs doesn't bother you, you must be crazy." Steven laughed and admitted that he did feel a little depressed sometimes. Later he confided that he got sudden attacks of misery that scared him. He was afraid that letting the misery in would overwhelm him so he couldn't work hard at getting better.

Talking to the psychologist about being scared and miserable made him feel better. The other guys at the center helped, too. They were like a club that you had to go through a horrible initiation to join. The club members kidded around, calling each other "gimp" and "crip." They competed for who took the worst flop or made the biggest mess. They told sick jokes and traded horror stories. But they knew how Steven felt inside because they felt the same way.

When he went home, he missed his sessions with the psychologist, and he missed the guys. He felt so alone. He didn't seem to speak the same language as his old friends anymore. They'd start talking about things he couldn't do anymore and trail off in embarrassment. Even Paul, his kid brother, was shy with him. His parents kept saying it was wonderful to have him home, and Steven couldn't bring himself to hurt their feelings by telling them how lonely and depressed he was. He pretended he was fine, and they pretended to believe him.

Steven felt like a stranger at home. Trisha was angry at her family for pushing her. Christopher had cut himself off from his friends to hide his illness. Each of them felt lost and alone. So when they were invited to join a support group for teens who had been injured or become sick, they all said "Yes."

A support group (also called a counseling group) is 4 to 12 people who have some problems in common and meet regularly to discuss them. The group usually gets together once a week with the same people attending each meeting. The number of meetings can be decided beforehand or left open-ended. The meetings are led by a psychologist, social worker, or peer counselor (a person who has previously dealt with the same problems and is now trained to help others).

A rap group (also called a self-help group) is less formal than a support group. There is no leader. The membership may be fixed, or it may change from session to session. A rap group is often part of a larger organization, with members of the organization going to meetings when problems come up and they need to discuss them.

Members of a support group or rap group share their experiences and talk about their feelings. The group shows them that they are not alone, that other people are struggling with the same problems and feelings. Members give one another emotional support and exchange information. Since they share many of the same problems, they can also share solutions. What works for one person may help someone else. A girl who is nervous about returning to school on crutches needs to hear how someone else handled it. Finding out about a wheelchair basketball team can get a boy back into sports. Although not all problems have solutions, it helps just to talk with people who are going through the same things.

Steven, Trisha, and Christopher joined a support group that met at the rehab center once a week for an hour and a half. It had six members, three boys and three girls, and was led by a social worker. Trisha, at 14, was the youngest member, and Chris, at 18, was the oldest. All of them had recently become disabled or sick. They were all coming to the center as outpatients for physical therapy or occupational therapy. The group met after their PT or OT sessions.

The social worker opened the first meeting. "I'm Ben, your group leader. I'll see that everyone gets a chance to speak. I'll ask some questions and summarize some of what's said. What you want to discuss is up to you. Being sick or disabled touches every part of your lives, so talk about whatever concerns you. Anything goes. And what you say stays in this room. I won't repeat a word to anyone, and neither must you. Don't discuss the meetings with your parents or friends or even with other group members if you meet outside. Any questions? Then let's start by going around the room and introducing ourselves. You might tell a little about what brought you here." He nodded to Trisha. "Will you go first?"

Trisha told about her accident. She complained that everything was always worse than the doctors and her family led her to expect. The cast and brace had just come off, but her arm and leg were as weak as cooked spaghetti. And they hurt. PT just made the pain worse. "Everyone tells me I'm lucky I'm going to get better. But I don't feel lucky. They say I shouldn't feel sorry for myself. But I do!" Then she was ashamed in front of the blind girl and the boy in the wheelchair, but they nodded as though they understood.

Ben asked the blind girl to go next. She just said, "I'm Yoko, and my guide dog is Blackie." Ben didn't push her to say more. He nodded to a boy with one arm.

"I'm Maurice. I had bone cancer, and they cut off my arm just above my elbow to cure it. They say I'm lucky the cancer is gone and I have enough of my real arm left to make fitting and using a false arm easier. But I sure don't feel lucky."

Steven didn't wait for Ben's nod. "I'm supposed to be lucky because my hip muscles work and I'm learning to walk in long braces. I can't stand that 'lucky' garbage."

There was a babble of voices agreeing that they couldn't stand it either. A girl who looked as though there wasn't anything wrong with her said, "If you died, they'd say you were lucky to have a nice coffin. My name is Carmen, and I have asthma. People think that asthma isn't a serious disease, that you just have fits of coughing or wheezing. My asthma was like that most of my life, but in the past six months I was rushed to the hospital twice to keep from choking to death. It's real scary."

Christopher was the last to introduce himself. "I'm Chris, and I have MS. I was iffy about this group. I wasn't sure I wanted to be with . . . but now I'm glad I joined."

Ben asked, "How do the rest of you feel about being in a group of people who have disabilities?"

It turned out that, except for Steven and Yoko, they'd all been leery of being with people who were "too disabled." Steven said he'd felt that way when he started at the rehab center. First he tried to keep to himself. Then he made friends with the paras. Then with the quads. Then he realized it didn't make any difference. People were people. Carmen said it was the same with all kinds of prejudice. When you get to know people, you forget whether they are black or white or green.

The hour and a half passed quickly. As they left, Chris watched Blackie lead Yoko out of the room. Every time his vision blurred—or he thought it did—he was terrified of going blind. How did Yoko stand it? Maybe if she told the group what it was like to be blind, he wouldn't be so scared. Yoko had hardly said a word during the meeting. He hoped she wouldn't be so shy next time.

Both support groups and rap groups give their members a sense of belonging and a safe place to air their feelings. The members of a leaderless rap group give one another understanding and support and serve as sounding boards for one another's ideas. But a support group with a leader can go deeper. Its members also discover why they feel and act the way they do. They figure out what choices they have and what they really want. As they recognize which of their feelings or habits are getting in the way of what they want, they develop new and better ways of solving problems. They grow and change.

The group leader's job goes beyond giving everyone a chance to talk and seeing that they don't get into fights if they disagree. He focuses the discussion and helps the group members say what they mean. When Chris was embarrassed to say he hadn't wanted to be with disabled people, Ben brought the issue out into the open. That gave Chris a chance to look at the way he felt and to see if it made sense. It also encouraged the rest of the group to examine their own feelings—feelings they might not have been aware of.

The leader helps the group discover what they think, feel, and want. It may seem strange that people often don't know what they feel, but it is true. Take a simple example: You are sitting home on a Sunday afternoon feeling bored. When a friend calls to ask if you'd like to go ice skating, you realize that skating is just what you're in the mood for. The group leader functions like that friend. He steps in at the right time with the right question.

Each member comes into the group with his or her own usual ways of acting. One person may be social and outgoing and love crowds and action while someone else is quiet and shy. When trouble strikes, one person gets angry, another feels sorry for herself, another rolls up his sleeves and meets the trouble head on. People's own behavior patterns feel so natural to them that they assume that the way they behave is the right and only way. When they act the same way in the group as they do in the rest of their lives, the group shows them how others see them. This feedback is not always pleasant, but it helps the group members discover new and better ways of thinking and behaving.

Trisha expected life to be easy, and she felt sorry for herself when it wasn't. During the first group sessions, the others sympathized with her disappointment about how long it was taking her to get well. She expected more sympathy when she complained that PT was too hard. But Steven said, "PT is supposed to be hard. If you don't push your muscles to do more and more, they'll never get strong."

Annoyed, Trisha answered, "Everyone doesn't have to push themselves twenty-four hours a day the way you do."

Steven snapped back, "Neither do they have to sit around whining the way you do."

"I don't whine!"

Steven turned to the others, "Does Trisha whine?"

Carmen nodded, and Maurice said, "She sure does."

Yoko was the peacemaker. "My father taught me that the middle road is best. It's all right to feel sorry for ourselves sometimes, but that shouldn't stop us from attempting difficult things."

Chris asked, "Can we do both? When I'm doing water therapy or eating whole grains, I feel like I have some control over my body and my life. But when I get even a little symptom—like my eyes blur for a few minutes—I think nothing I do will keep me from getting worse. Then I just want to give up."

Ben asked, "Do you give up?"

Chris shook his head. "I did for a while after my second attack, but now when I want to hole up in my room, I make myself study or practice **t'ai chi.** I'm taking t'ai chi—Chinese shadow boxing—in school for gym. Doing the slow exercises calms me and makes me feel better."

Steven asked Trisha, "Are you learning something?"

She answered, "Are you?" and everyone laughed.

They were all learning from one another. When the physical therapist told Trisha she'd only get out of PT what she put into it, Trisha felt put upon. She felt unjustly accused when her sister said she used her injuries to avoid anything she didn't want to do. But when her friends in the group called her a whiner, it got to her. She told herself she used to be cheerful like Carmen before the accident. She'd show them she could still be that way.

Steven kept thinking about Yoko's "middle road." His psychologist had told him that he pushed himself to keep from giving in to despair, but he didn't know what else to do. Look how depressed he got when he was home doing nothing. Now that he was back in school, going to PT three days a week, and working himself into exhaustion, the depression was gone. But maybe there was a middle road. Chris seemed to have found it.

Chris felt better about himself. With one question, Ben had shown him the difference between wanting to give up and actually doing it.

Yoko wondered if she could learn t'ai chi. Her cousin had done it for years. When she could still see, she liked to watch him because he looked so graceful and calm. Maybe he could teach her. Maybe t'ai chi would make her feel as calm as she pretended to be.

The support group at the rehab center had been organized to help its members deal with being sick or disabled. But it was also geared to helping them get in touch with their feelings and to their emotional growth. The members were encouraged to talk about their problems and achievements. Sharing their "bad" feelings and having them accepted by the group eased their shame and guilt. Sharing their successes boosted their self-esteem. And getting the group's reactions to their behavior spurred them to look for better ways to solve problems.

Because all the members were teens, they had to adjust to new disabilities at the same time that they were grappling with the normal physical and emotional changes of adolescence. They were trying to find out who they were and what they wanted to do with their lives while they tested what their disabilities would let them do.

Disabled teens ask themselves the same questions that all teens ask: Do I want to be independent or have other people do things for me? Can I do both at different times? If I fall on my face, who will pick up the pieces? Does having freedom mean not taking responsibility, or is it just the opposite? But disabled teens must ask themselves one more question: What about my disability?

All teens have conflicts between being independent and relying on their families. But being independent is harder if you are blind like Yoko or frequently hospitalized with asthma attacks like Carmen. All teens want to be accepted and liked for what they really are. But it is harder to be accepted when people see your wheelchair or guide dog before they see you.

For the year that their group met, Trisha, Christopher, Steven, Yoko, Carmen, and Maurice looked at their disabilities and their lives. They talked about school and the kind of jobs they wanted later on, about clothes and sports, recreation, learning to drive, and traveling. They discussed friends and dating and sex and being different. They talked about their mothers and fathers, their sisters and brothers. They spoke about how they felt about themselves. As the group went on, they developed skills in recognizing and handling their problems. They became freer and related better to other people. And they felt better about themselves.

CHAPTER 7

School

The Education for All Handicapped Children Act of 1975 guarantees all elementary- , junior-high- , and high-school students "a free and appropriate public education" in the "least restrictive environment." This means that students who have disabilities should be mainstreamed wherever possible. They should attend regular classes, preferably in the school they would ordinarily go to. When disabled students need special classes, the law says that they should join the able-bodied students in as many school and extracurricular activities as possible. (Being blind rules out the football team, but it doesn't interfere with singing in the chorus.) The school system must provide any transportation, equipment, and services that disabled students need to help them to learn and to be part of school life.

After an accident or during an acute illness, students are often too sick to go to school. Under the law, the school system arranges for them to attend classes in the hospital or to have a teacher come to their homes. But students return to school as soon as they can, even if they have been left with disabilities and need extra help to go back to school.

Getting to school on their own is difficult or impossible for some disabled students, so the law says they must have free transportation. In towns where all students get bus service, able-bodied and disabled students often ride together. In cities where most students walk or take a public bus or subway to school, each disabled student's needs are examined separately. Of the six members of the support group, Maurice and Carmen travel to school as they did before they became ill. Maurice walks the six blocks to his school, and Carmen takes the subway to hers. Yoko and Steven are picked up at their homes by school buses. Steven's bus is equipped with a wheelchair lift. Trisha was also eligible for a school bus because she was still on crutches when she went back to school. But the public bus stops at her corner, and her friend Beth agreed to call for her on the way to the bus. So Trisha rides with Beth and her other friends. Christopher has already graduated from high school, so he is not covered by the education law.

When disabled students reach school, they have to be able to get inside. Then they need to go from class to class, up to the gym and down to the auditorium. The school must be accessible to them. Someone like Trisha, who is on crutches, needs an elevator to get to the upper floors. She was also given a pass that allowed her extra time going from class to class.

It takes more than an elevator and a pass to make a school accessible to Steven, who uses a wheelchair. Three steps up to the front door are an impossible barrier unless a ramp is built. Then the door may be too heavy to open from a sitting position. If the classroom seats are bolted down, the aisles are often too narrow for a wheelchair. Or there may be no place to park the chair without being in everyone else's way. Standard tables in the science labs are too high to work at, and bathrooms with narrow stalls are a special problem. Since Steven's school was not wheelchair accessible, he was transferred to a school that was.

Some students need special equipment to help them learn. Adaptive equipment can be as simple as large-print books, or as sophisticated as computers, talking calculators, or voice-recognition machines. A print enlarger or a Kurzweil (voice print) machine in the school library makes it possible for partly sighted students to use the library books. A portable FM listening system can help hard-of-hearing students follow class lessons. A tape recorder lets a blind student or one with weak hands take notes in class. Tape recorders can also help students with learning disabilities by letting them replay lessons at home until they master the work.

Good equipment can help disabled students succeed in school. Good teachers can help even more. A good teacher arranges the class seating so that students with hearing or vision problems sit in front and someone who uses a wheelchair is not stuck in a back corner. The teacher faces hard-of-hearing students when she speaks so they can read her lips. She encourages students who stutter to speak in class and waits patiently for them to get their words out. She sends work home when a chronically ill student has an attack and allows him extra time for assignments when he isn't feeling well. A good teacher gives disabled students all the help they need, but she expects them to do their work well. She knows that having a disability does not rule out having many other abilities. She holds disabled students to the same high standards as the rest of the class.

Some schools run workshops for teachers who have disabled students in their classes. Like many of the interviewees in the Harris Poll, teachers may be uncomfortable around people with disabilities. They may carry false pictures of "the disabled" in their minds. They may pity disabled students and treat them differently from the rest of the class. The workshops must change these attitudes so the teachers can learn better ways of teaching.

The first thing that teachers' workshops stress is that disabled and able-bodied students are much more alike than they are different. Having a disability does not make someone into a superstudent who always strives to do his or her very best. Neither does it make that student a pathetic weakling who can't be expected to achieve anything. Some disabled students are hard workers; others are lazy. Some are quick and bright; others take longer to catch on. Some are quiet; others always have something to say. In other words, they are like able-bodied students.

Both able-bodied and disabled students sometimes need more help than their regular classroom teachers can give them. So schools provide tutors, guidance counselors, psychologists, vocational counselors, social workers, educational evaluators, physical and occupational therapists, speech therapists, doctors, and nurses. Not all schools have all these services. A typical high school will have a tutoring center, a full-time guidance counselor or college adviser, and a psychologist or social worker two or three days a week. If other specialists are needed, they are called in or the student is referred to them.

Sometimes a guidance counselor can solve a problem alone. For example, arranging a lighter program for a student whose chemotherapy for cancer leaves him weak and tired. Sometimes a teacher or guidance counselor refers students for evaluation to find out what kind of schooling is best for them. A parent can also request an evaluation. Students who have been hospitalized are usually evaluated before they return to school to see if they can return to their regular classes.

As part of a full evaluation, a social worker talks to the student and the parent or legal guardian about school and family problems. The social worker also gets a medical report from the student's doctor. A psychologist interviews the student and tests his or her intelligence, motor skills, and emotional health. An educational evaluator tests math and reading skills. If necessary, there are examinations by a speech therapist, neurologist, eye doctor, or hearing specialist.

When all the information has been gathered, the student and parent join the teacher, psychologist, and other team members in an educational planning conference. They discuss whether the student should stay in his regular classes, what extra help he needs to do well there, or if he should transfer to a special class or program. If the school does not have the special program, the student can change schools. But no student can be placed in a special program without a parent's consent.

Yoko was evaluated when she began to lose her sight. At the conference, the team recommended a program for visually impaired (partly sighted or blind) students where she would learn to read Braille along with her other school subjects. They suggested she start immediately, but it meant transferring to a school a distance away. Yoko pleaded with her parents not to send her. She couldn't bear to leave her friends and start in a strange place in the middle of the year. Her parents worked out a compromise with the team. Since Yoko could still see fairly well, she would finish the school year with her friends and begin the new program in the fall. Meanwhile, she would learn Braille after school.

By the time Yoko started in the visually impaired program, she had gotten used to the idea. Between what she learned in the program and her occupational therapy at the rehab center, she was independent enough to attend regular classes when she went to college three years later.

Steven's rehab center was attached to a large hospital, so he attended the hospital school while he was at the center. Youngsters who are hospitalized for more than a week are referred to a hospital teacher. She meets the students and then contacts their schools to find out what they are supposed to be learning and what textbooks they are using. If she doesn't already have the books, she gets them from the school. The hospital teacher will probably plan her own lessons for younger children and arrange to get older students' assignments from their schools. The idea is to teach students what they would be learning in their regular classes so they won't be behind when they return to school. If necessary, a hospital teacher can give midterms, finals, and special tests like Regents exams.

Hospital schools work on a regular school year. Since Steven's accident happened during summer vacation, he did not start classes until he was in the rehab center for two weeks. The hospital school had three teachers assigned to it by the city school system. One teacher worked with all the elementary students, one with the junior-high students, and one with the high-school students. There were seven other high-school students in Steven's class. Two were from his SCI unit. They were in the class with him for the whole time he was there. The rest of the students were from the hospital. They came and went, most staying only for a week or two.

The teacher taught all subjects except advanced math. A volunteer came in once a week for that. The teacher worked with students individually or in small groups. She took attendance and gave homework, as in any other class. The class met for two hours a day, but some students were too sick to stay the whole time even though the classroom was equipped with oxygen and IV hookups. The teacher gave them their work in bed in the morning, and they came to class for an hour—or less—in the afternoon.

Steven attended the hospital class for two and a half months. He'd always been a so-so student. His teachers used to say he could do better if he put his mind to it, but he'd been too busy running around to concentrate on studying. Now that he couldn't run around, he surprised himself with how well he did on his midterms. In the past, when his parents talked about college, he'd always said it wasn't for him. Now he was changing his mind.

Before Steven left the rehab center, his teacher had a conference with the rest of the rehab team and his parents. The team recommended that Steven finish out the term on home instruction. A teacher would come to his house every day. That way he could get used to being home and getting around the neighborhood before he started school again. He couldn't go back to his old school because it wasn't wheelchair accessible, and it would be easier for him to start in a new school at the beginning of a new term.

His parents asked Steven what he thought about the plan. He said it was okay. The truth was that he was too uptight about going home to think about anything else.

He was glad not to have to worry about starting school at the same time.

Like Steven, Trisha attended a hospital class, although she only went for a short while. Her teacher, doctor, and therapist discussed whether she should go back to school when she left the hospital. Students often return to school with an arm or leg in a cast. But besides the cast, Trisha wore a brace that kept her from sitting up straight, and she couldn't put weight on her leg. So they decided to put her on home instruction until the cast and brace came off.

Elementary school pupils usually get five hours a week—one hour a day—of classes in a hospital and the same amount of home instruction. High-school students get ten hours a week in the hospital or at home. Like hospital teachers, home instruction teachers keep in touch with the students' schools and work from the school assignments as much as they can. One teacher usually teaches all subjects, although a special teacher may come in once or twice a week if a student is taking advanced courses like physics or calculus.

Trisha was a high-school freshman, so a teacher came to her house for two hours every day. One of her sisters picked up Trisha's assignments from school, and the home teacher worked on them with her. The teacher also gave Trisha homework: readings in her textbooks and written work that she did on the computer with her left hand. Her sisters went over the homework and explained anything she didn't understand. When Trisha finally went back to school, she was able to keep up with her classes.

Trisha and Steven were put on home instruction after a hospital stay, but students don't have to be hospitalized first. They can have a home teacher if they are out sick for more than a week. In either case, home instruction is meant to be temporary. Students can keep up with what they would be learning in school, but they miss getting out every day and being with their friends. They may feel lonely or even become depressed. So the home teacher sends them back to school just as soon as they are ready.

The Education for All Handicapped Children Act guarantees all students a free public education, as well as any services they need, until they graduate from high school. Disabled students have until age 21 to complete high school, but the education law no longer covers them when they graduate.

College students are covered under Section 504 of the Rehabilitation Act of 1973. Unlike the education law, the Rehabilitation Act does not provide free schooling or services. Instead, it forbids colleges to discriminate against students who are disabled. Colleges must use the same standards—like grade averages and SAT scores—for disabled and able-bodied students. Scholarships, loans, and other financial aid must be the same for both.

The rehabilitation law also says that colleges must be accessible to disabled students. Accessibility means building ramps, installing elevators, and providing some lower lab tables and larger bathroom stalls in school buildings. It means making over some dorm rooms: lowering closet bars, removing door sills, etc. Although some colleges have been made completely accessible, it is too difficult or expensive to change some older buildings in other colleges. So the law lets the colleges make "alternate arrangements" for disabled students. If a student who uses a wheelchair wants to take a class that meets in a room he can't get to, he will be switched to another section of the same course. If there isn't another section, the class will be moved to an accessible room.

Making a college accessible, however, involves more than building ramps or providing handicapped parking spaces. It also means having adaptive equipment like reading machines, Braille typewriters, and special computers in the library, computer center, etc. It means allowing disabled students to use tape recorders or Braillers in class and giving them large print, extra time, or oral exams when necessary. It means providing people who can read to blind students and sign language interpreters for deaf students. It means having tutoring and counseling available. Disabled students may need to take fewer courses each term and graduate in five or six years instead of the usual four. Those who live in the dorms may need personal care aides to help them wash and dress in the morning and get to bed at night.

The difference between the education law and Section 504 of the rehabilitation law reflects the difference between high school and college. Until you graduate from high school, the school system takes responsibility for you. It provides the education and services you need. When you go to college, you take responsibility for yourself. You must ask for any special services, and you may have to pay for some of them yourself or get government aid. Most colleges have an office of disabled student services to help students succeed in college. The counselors tell students what services are available and help them arrange for what they need. But disabled services counselors do not go looking for students to help. It is the students' responsibility to contact the office.

Christopher had read about disabled students services in his college catalog. His mother had urged him to go see them, but he didn't want any part of anything with the word "disabled" in it. However, after he'd been in the support group for a while, he changed his mind.

The counselor agreed with Chris that there was no reason to tell his professors about his illness while he was feeling well. She gave him a form for make-up tests and extra time for term papers if he had another attack. She suggested he join the disabled students' club. On his way out of the office, Chris thought of Steven. "My friend uses a wheelchair. What should he do about going to college?" The counselor told him the college had a summer program to introduce disabled high-school juniors and seniors to college life. She gave him the information for Steven.

Deciding whether to go to college and what college to attend are major decisions. High-school students ask themselves: Do I want to live at home or go away to college? Do I prefer a large city college or a small one in the country? What do I want to study? What kind of career am I preparing for? What will my education cost? Disabled students ask additional questions: Am I independent enough to live in a dorm? If I live at home, how will I get to school and back? How accessible are the school buildings? What extracurricular activities are available to me?

If Steven decides to go to college, he should start collecting information in his junior year in high school. He should send for college catalogs and write to the disabled-students services offices of the colleges he is interested in. When he has narrowed down his choices to a few schools, he should visit each of them and wheel himself around the campus, sit in on a class, eat in the cafeteria, and inspect the dorms. He should look at the library, the health services, and the Student Union. If possible, he should talk to students on campus who use wheelchairs and ask how they manage. While it is a good idea for all students to visit the colleges they are considering attending, it is especially important for students with disabilities to make sure that the school is accessible to them and has the services they need.

Whether or not Steven decides to go to college, or if he can't decide, he should contact the local **Vocational Rehabilitation (VR)** office while he is still in high school. (His school guidance counselor can call for him.) Vocational Rehabilitation is a national program to help people with disabilities train for and get jobs. It provides counseling to help them decide what kind of work they want to do and to deal with any problems they might have in achieving their goals. VR also gives them financial aid for job training. That can involve on-the-job training or attending a vocational or technical school, a work/study program, college, or even law or medical school. Steven and a vocational counselor would work out what was best for him.

CHAPTER 8

Friends

School is more than a place to learn math and science and social studies. It is also a center of social life. Students talk to their classmates before and after classes in the halls, in the cafeteria, and on the bus. They join a club or write for the school magazine or sing in the chorus or play on a team. They meet people and make friends.

Some teens are eager to be popular. Others are content with a few good friends. But everyone wants to be accepted for who he or she is. Nobody wants to be shut out. Unfortunately, people who are seen as "different" are often avoided or ignored—whether their difference is their race, religion, family background, or disability. In school, their classmates may act as if they weren't there. Or they may be included in casual classroom conversation but left behind at lunchtime or when people get together after school. Disabled students may find it hard to make friends.

There are several kinds of friendship, and disabled teens can have trouble with one or more of them. Casual friends are part of one another's lives because they are thrown together, often because they live on the same block or are in the same class. When they meet, they chat easily about their teachers or who will win the playoffs. They are willing to help each other if it isn't too much trouble. A casual friend will let you copy her class notes after you've been out sick. Or he will borrow a drip pan when he's changing the oil in his car. But casual friends don't seek one another out to go shopping or play sports. They don't invite one another to parties. If one of them moves away or if they are in different classes next term, they become casually friendly with other people.

Pals have more in common than the same neighborhood or class. They share some activity that they both enjoy or that they think is important: playing music, dirt biking, collecting old movies, or doing volunteer work. They may belong to a band that practices twice a week, go biking most Saturdays, or get together occasionally to watch a tape. But their time together is spent in the shared activity, and that is usually what they talk about. If one of them can't continue with the activity, the friendship will probably peter out.

Close friends often live in the same neighborhood or go to the same school. They have fun together, sharing activities that they both enjoy. But they also just talk. They talk about who they saw yesterday and what pests their brothers are and whether they should go to college and what their parents expect of them. They confide in each other and support each other. When a girl breaks up with her boyfriend, her close friend listens to her doubts and assures her that she did the right thing. The friend listens and doesn't repeat what she hears. When a guy dents the fender of his father's car, his close friend lends him the money to have it fixed. When a girl gets a part in the play or a boy is accepted by the team—or the other way around—their close friends cheer them on. And if they were too scared to try out, their friends understand. Good friends know that you are not perfect, and they like you anyway. They are the ones who stick by you when you are sick or hurt.

Close friendships don't suddenly appear out of the blue. They grow out of casual friendships or shared activities. Two girls who sit together in English class are casual friends until they discover that they both like poetry. When one goes to a reading by feminist poets, she asks the other along. They are soon fast friends. Or two guys who own motorcycles get together to work on their bikes. They talk as they tinker and find that they're interested in a lot of the same things. So they hang out together, going from being pals to close friends.

Studies show that disabled teens have fewer friends than able-bodied teens. Other people see the disability before they see the person who has it. Some people never get past the disability because they want friends who are attractive, and a disability is not considered attractive. Disabled people usually have to make the first moves and go more than halfway to make friends. However, if they have been disabled since birth or early childhood, they have experienced some rejections because of their disability. As a result, they may be shy about reaching out for friendship.

Even when they are friendly and outgoing, disabled teens may not have many opportunities to make friends with able-bodied teens. If they are in special classes, they are cut off from casual contacts with able-bodied students, especially if their disabilities keep them from taking part in after-school or outside activities. If they are mainstreamed, disabled teens may find themselves ignored by classmates who are not sure how to treat them.

Casual class friendships between disabled and able-bodied students often don't carry past the classroom door. Imagine four girls leaving Spanish class together and heading to the cafeteria for lunch. Hoping to beat the line, three of them run down the stairs. The fourth uses a wheelchair. She must go to the end of the hall and wait for the elevator. It takes a long time to come. When she finally gets to the cafeteria, her friends are already eating with some other girls at a crowded table. There doesn't seem to be room for her, and she is shy about pushing in. So she ends up eating by herself. Or imagine three guys standing around after class arguing the Mets' chances this year. One of them is hard-of-hearing. Because the others don't look at him when they talk, he misses most of what they are saying. After he asks "What?" twice, he just stands quietly.

The able-bodied students aren't cruel, just thoughtless. They forget that some people have special needs. If the girl in the wheelchair said, "Save me a place at the table," or the boy with the hearing problem said, "Look at me when you talk so I can read your lips," their friends would probably have done so. But it is embarrassing to keep reminding people of your disability. So some disabled teens keep to themselves, and some look to others with disabilities for friendship.

Many able-bodied people assume that disabled people prefer having disabled friends. They reason that people choose friends who are like themselves. That is usually true. Ask yourself: How many of your friends are much older or younger than you? How many are a different color? How many are of the opposite sex? (This refers to friendship, not dating.) The answers are probably "None" or "Not many." So if you feel that all people with disabilities are pretty much alike, you expect them to be friends with one another. If you think that some of them are like you, you will probably make friends with them.

When the support group discussed friends, all the members felt that their illness or accident affected their friendships in some way. Christopher, who has MS, and Carmen, with serious asthma, had both wondered whether to tell their friends about their illnesses or to try to hide them. They arrived at different answers. Chris didn't tell anyone. "I don't want people to feel sorry for me or treat me differently."

Carmen said, "If people don't know you're sick, they think you're weird. I was with this girl who was smoking, and I asked her to put out her cigarette. Because I didn't explain that smoke gives me an asthma attack, she thought I was being a pill. She kept puffing away until I started to wheeze. Since then I tell people if there's a reason. Of course, my close friends know all about it. I tal' to them when I'm scared or just sick of being sick. Didn't you need a friend to talk to when you found out you had MS?"

Chris shook his head. "My best friend was going away to college. What good would it have done to confide in him when he was leaving soon and I'd hardly see him anymore? Besides, it bothered me that he could go away to school and I couldn't. When he talked about dorm rooms and meal plans, I felt like he was rubbing it in. His college talk made me so mad that I didn't want to see him. I made excuses when he called or dropped in."

Ben, the group leader, asked Chris if he was still angry at his friend. Chris said he wasn't. "I realize it wasn't his fault I couldn't go away to school, and he didn't know how hard it was for me to listen to his plans. Maybe I'll call him when he's home for vacation. If he isn't too mad at me for how I acted, I'd like to be friends again. But I still don't want to tell him I have MS."

Maurice said, "Friends can't handle it when you're sick. When I was in the hospital, my friends acted like I'd dropped off the edge of the earth. None of them came to visit me. Oh, a few phoned, but they didn't know what to say, and they hung up as soon as they could."

Trisha disagreed. "My friend Beth wasn't like that. She came to the hospital twice and she called me a lot, and we talked on the phone the way we always did."

Maurice answered, "Maybe Beth is a better friend than mine were. Or maybe it's because you were in a car accident. Cancer is different. It scares friends off because they think you're going to die. If they do talk to you, they never say the word 'cancer.' It's like they'll catch it if they say it. And bad as it is with cancer, AIDS is worse. I knew a kid in the hospital who got AIDS from a blood transfusion, but the one friend who called him talked like he brought it on himself."

There was a silence. Then Steven said, "I used to hang out with a bunch of guys from the neighborhood. They came to visit when I was first hospitalized. They cracked jokes to cheer me up and told me all the neighborhood gossip. But it didn't take long for them to run out of jokes and gossip, and they never came to the rehab center. After I was home again, we all went out to eat. I could see they hadn't expected the hassle of getting my wheelchair in and out of the car and up the step at the diner entrance, but they pretended they didn't mind. When we got our burgers, they started talking about roller blades.

Then they looked at me and changed the subject. Only there wasn't much else to talk about. We didn't have anything in common anymore. It was weeks before they called me to go out again, and they were relieved when I said I had to visit my grandmother. I don't blame them. I didn't really want to see them either. One good thing about changing schools is that I don't run into them. I'd rather be with people who didn't know me when I was a speed demon, who think this is the way I always was."

Ben asked, "Have you made new friends in school?"

"Not really. Before my accident, I just naturally got along with people. And I made friends right away in the rehab center. But now in school it's like there's an invisible wall around me. The other kids say 'Hi' or hold the door open for me, but they don't seem to know what to say to me. I don't know how to talk to them either."

Yoko told Steven, "That's how it was with me when I lost my sight. Now I have friends in the visually impaired program at school. They're blind like me. Trisha and Carmen and Chris and even Maurice can be friends with 'normal' people. But our disabilities are too bad. We have to make friends with our own kind."

There was a storm of protest. Trisha said that people were people, and if you liked someone, her disability didn't matter. Maurice said that Trisha believed that because she didn't have a permanent disability. He said it was easy for her to talk because she was going to be normal again. Chris said Trisha should be right, but unfortunately the world wasn't like that. He asked how Steven's classmates could find out if they liked him if they never got to know him.

Steven just listened. When Ben asked him what he thought, he said, "I don't like feeling that I can only have friends who use wheelchairs—especially when there are so few in my school. But neither do I want friends I can't keep up with. I can't think of anything worse than sitting in my wheelchair watching my friends play sports. Maybe if the guys from the rehab center had kept in touch . . . now that's something that really bothers me. I know some of them live out of town, but Aaron is here in the city. Aaron was my best buddy in the rehab center, and he never called me after he went home."

Trisha hadn't forgiven Steven for calling her a whiner. She got even by asking, "If Aaron was your best friend, why didn't *you* call *him?*"

Steven had thought of calling Aaron, but his experience with his old friends had left him feeling unsure of himself. He was afraid that the same thing would happen with Aaron now that they weren't in rehab together anymore. But he was not going to admit that to Trisha. He said, "I've been meaning to. I'll call Aaron tonight."

Some of the same problems that interfere with disabled teens making friends also keep them from dating. One problem is lack of opportunity. Like close friendships, dates often arise out of casual friendships. When a boy and a girl talk together in class, they may carry on the conversation over a cup of coffee. Then they may decide to go skating or see a movie. Shared activities like rehearsing for a play, being on the debating team, or working on a recycling drive can also lead to dating. If disabled teens are not part of casual classroom contacts or extracurricular activities, they have few chances to meet people to date.

Friends of the same sex are another source of dates. A girl makes a party, or a boy asks his girlfriend to fix up his friend with her friend. Because disabled teens often have fewer friends than able-bodied teens, they are less likely to go to parties or to double date.

Even when disabled teens have the opportunity to meet people they might want to date, there are additional problems. If physical appearance plays a part in forming friendships, it is even more important in dating. People who are physically attractive are more likely to be asked out on dates or to be accepted if they do the asking. So all teens wonder: Am I pretty (or handsome), charming, sexy? Are boys (or girls) attracted to me? Will I find the special someone I can love? Will she (or he) love me back? These questions are harder for teens with disabilities.

When able-bodied teens compare themselves to the models and actors who are our sexual ideals, they worry that they don't measure up. They feel that they are too short or too tall, too fat or too thin, that their skin is spotty or their nose isn't right. They may worry that they aren't attractive to the opposite sex, that they won't be popular, or that nobody will love them. Disabled teens, who rarely see disabled models or actors, may feel that people with disabilities cannot be desirable. They compare themselves to the able-bodied, and the more severe their disability is, the less desirable they are likely to feel.

Without giving it much thought, many able-bodied people assume that the disabled are not interested in sex. They also think that a person with a disability who wants love should find it with another disabled person. An able-bodied girl who is friendly with a girl who uses crutches is seen as a good and caring person. If she spends time with a disabled boy, people will usually assume that they are friends. If it becomes clear that they are dating, people may wonder why she can't attract an able-bodied boy. A boy who dates a disabled girl may be judged even more harshly.

Like friendship, dating was discussed in the support group. This time Christopher and Carmen agreed on not telling their dates about their illnesses. Chris said, "I met a girl in school that I really like, and she likes me. We see a lot of each other, and we talk about everything, but not about that. She thinks I'm smart and strong. Maybe she's half right. And maybe it wouldn't change anything if I started toppling over. But I'm scared to take the chance. Right now my balance is better. I think the PT is helping. But if I have another attack . . . well, maybe I'll tell her then."

Carmen said, "If she really cares about you, she'll stick by you. If she doesn't, you'll just have to say it was good while it lasted. I don't have that kind of problem because I don't get serious about any guy. I just like to have fun, and fun guys don't want to hear about sickness. So if I cough or wheeze I laugh at my 'allergy.'"

Maurice said bitterly, "It's fine for you two. You look normal, so you can date normal people. But normal girls don't want to date me because I have only one arm."

Carmen answered, "Maybe it's not your arm. Maybe it's the chip on your shoulder."

"Sure. Blame me. But you date a lot. How many disabled guys have you gone out with?"

Carmen thought about it. "Actually, none. But I would if I liked the guy."

"Ha!"

"I'd go out with Steven in a second. He's good-looking and he's fun." She threw Steven an exaggerated come-on look.

Before Steven's accident, girls had often flirted with

him. Carmen made him feel that he hadn't changed so much after all. He laughed and said, "Be careful what you offer. I may take you up on that date in two months when I get my wheels. Car wheels, that is. My parents promised me a car with hand controls for my birthday."

"Why should we wait two months? My cousin is appearing at this comedy club Saturday night. I'm dying to go see him, but I hate sitting alone. Why don't you come with me? My cousin would drive us. You don't have to think of it as a date."

Everyone was looking at Steven. He smiled and said, "It's a date."

CHAPTER 9

Sports and Recreation

S teven had told Trisha he would call Aaron, and he did. Aaron was glad to hear from him. He said he'd meant to keep in touch, but he'd developed a **pressure sore.** Pressure sores are mean things. If a paraplegic doesn't take very good care of his skin (and sometimes even if he does), a place where a bone presses against the wheelchair can open up into a deep ulcer that takes weeks of rest or even surgery to close. Aaron said, "It's healed now, but I missed a lot of basketball practice."

Steven said, "I remember you were thinking of joining the wheelchair basketball team the recreational counselor told us about. Don't you find it slow after playing the real thing?"

"Slow! If you think it's slow, come and watch us."

"I might do that. If my dad will drive me."

His father drove him and stayed to see the game. Lately Steven and his father had been doing things together. It was the one good thing to come out of the accident. As they watched the fast and furious action, Steven said, "I thought the game was going to be slow. Those guys are animals!"

His father laughed. He was a gym teacher, so he'd known what to expect. "Wheelchair basketball was started after World War II by a group of paralyzed war veterans. They were no cream puffs. And neither is anyone else who plays it. You have to be in top shape to push your chair at that speed and then turn and stop on a dime—all with one hand while you're dribbling the ball and shooting with the other hand."

Before the 1940s, most people with spinal cord injuries did not live long enough to think about sports. Advances in medicine during World War II changed the situation. In 1945, paralyzed war veterans in a California rehab program were bored with their physical therapy. They invented wheelchair basketball as a way of having fun while they built their strength and endurance. Organized sports for the disabled have grown from those first basketball games into a worldwide movement. Today disabled athletes are found in every sport from archery to scuba diving and in every place from the school gym to the Paralympics.

Like other sports for the disabled, wheelchair basketball is played with the same basic rules as stand-up basketball. The court size and basket height are the same. However, players get two pushes per dribble and five seconds in the free throw line instead of three. A player's chair is considered part of him or her, and roughness against the chair is roughness against the person in it. Charging and blocking are illegal. Wheelchair basketball also has a *team balance* requirement.

To keep sports for the disabled fair to all, the National Wheelchair Athletic Association (NWAA) measures each player's disabilities. It takes into account the level of spinal injury or amputation, muscle strength, balance, etc., and assigns each player to a class. There are three classes for basketball. Class I is for the most severe disabilities, and Class III is for the least. To have team balance in a basketball game, the class numbers of the five players on the court must not add up to more than 12.

The NWAA has eight classes for swimming and seven for other sports. In individual sports like swimming, skiing, and road racing, people compete against members of their own class. Steven, who has good upper body strength and balance and the use of his hip muscles, would be in Class III for basketball and Class IV for other sports.

Aaron invited Steven to try out for the basketball team. Steven's father urged him to do it. He said sports were good exercise. They improve muscle and heart strength, breathing, circulation, and digestion. He had read that people with spinal cord injuries who were active in sports had less than half the health problems of those who weren't. And sports were social. Steven was alone in the house too much; playing basketball would get him out to have fun with other people.

Steven said he'd give it a try.

Being on the basketball team did all the things his father promised. The training was great exercise. Fast dribbling around a track and sprinting up ramps built his strength, stamina, and concentration. And he liked the speed of it. He also enjoyed being with Aaron and the other guys. They were a bunch of practical jokers, and Steven fell right in with the silly things they did. Since his accident, his life had been all struggle and work. It was great to have fun again.

Basketball made him feel better about himself. Unlike Christopher, whose feelings of being worthwhile came from being smart, much of Steven's self-esteem was tied up with being strong and daring. (This was one reason he worked so hard in PT.) Playing basketball proved that he was still athletic, that he was all right.

After playing for a few months, he felt confident enough to look around for another sport. Although he was fast on the court, he wasn't that good at sinking baskets. And he'd never been keen on team sports. What he really wanted was a sport he could do on his own, one where he would have the freedom to train and compete when he wanted, and one that would get him out in the open air. He also didn't want a sport where he was only with people in wheelchairs. He found what he was looking for in road racing.

Wheelchair road racing has been growing in popularity since 1975, when the first wheelchair athlete entered the Boston Marathon. (In 1978 George Murray finished the marathon in his wheelchair ahead of the fastest foot runner.) Today races range from 100-meter track sprints to the 367-mile Midnight Sun Wheelchair Marathon that runs from Fairbanks to Anchorage in Alaska. Although some races—like the Midnight Sun—are for wheelers only, most wheelchair races are part of regular foot races in which the wheelchair athletes compete in a separate division.

In team sports like basketball and football, disabled athletes do not play able-bodied teams. Nor is there contact between them. But runners and wheelers see a lot of one another in road racing. Steven liked that. He joined a runner's club that also served wheelers. After he got his race chair, he entered a few races. But what he liked most was to zip down the waterside promenade in his race chair on a Saturday morning. He'd start off slowly to warm up. Then he'd pass the joggers and catch up with the runners and bikers. He'd greet people he knew and sometimes wheel alongside someone from the club for a while. Then he'd take off as fast as he could go. He knew that racing speed was 14 to 16 miles an hour, but he felt as though he were doing 100. He felt like a speed demon again.

Road racing helped Steven feel good about himself once more. Basketball worked for Aaron. Since disabled people are all different from one another, they choose different sports. Some prefer team sports like volleyball or softball. Others like to compete one-on-one in tennis or bowling. Still others are looking for recreation in golf or boating or for adventure in climbing mountains or piloting gliders. Today most sports are open to the disabled, and many sports have an organization devoted to helping people with disabilities take part.

Tennis is the fastest-growing sport for wheelers. Wheelchair tennis began in 1976 with exhibition matches between two players. Today more than 10,000 people in 30 countries play. Some are quadriplegics in power chairs. Since the rules are largely the same as for stand-up tennis, able-bodied and disabled friends can play together. The only difference is that wheelchair players get two bounces before the ball is called dead. The two-bounce rule lets wheelers chase drop shots and makes for a more interesting game.

If the tennis courts are all taken, there is racquetball or table tennis (Ping Pong). Wheelchair racquetball is newer than tennis and is not yet as popular, but people who play it love it. It is fast and fun, and they can beat able-bodied players. Although wheelchair racquetball has the same two-bounce rule as tennis, table tennis hasn't changed any rules for wheelchair players.

However, not everyone enjoys competitive sports. There are also many sports for disabled people looking for recreation without competition. Three of the most popular are horseback riding, skiing, and swimming. All three provide freedom and mobility. Wheelchair users can't usually go for a hike in the woods because the trails are too narrow and bumpy, but they can ride a horse along a trail or across the fields. In a wheelchair they look up at everyone else; on a horse, they are the same height as other riders. Many stables give riding lessons to the disabled and offer mounting ramps and adaptive saddles. Horseback riding is also used as recreational therapy for disabled youngsters to improve their coordination and balance. And controlling the horse gives them a sense of control over their environment.

Skiing is another sport that offers freedom to people with disabilities. What could be freer than speeding down a snowy mountain on a crisp winter day? People who have lost an arm or leg use outrigger ski poles with a small ski on the bottom. People who normally use wheelchairs ride a mono-ski. They sit a few feet off the ground on a chair attached to a single ski and use outrigger poles for balance and control. Mono-skiers can do everything other downhill skiers can. Part of the appeal of skiing is the social life in the ski lodge. Skiing can be part of a family vacation or a way to make new friends.

Unfortunately, skiing can be expensive, and it is often difficult to get to the slopes. Swimming is cheaper and more easily available. Besides community and Y pools, many high-school and college pools are open to the public in the evening. Because water buoys up the body, even severely disabled people can learn to swim. They are able to do things in the water that they can't manage on land.

Although swimming is good aerobic exercise, it puts less stress on the body than other aerobic sports. It also has a very low injury rate. Of course, swimming is a sport that can be shared with able-bodied friends or family members. If swimmers get bored with paddling around the pool or swimming laps, there are water exercise programs, water volleyball and polo, or swimming meets. Come summer, the lake or beach beckons. And for the adventurous, there is scuba diving.

Whatever their favorite sport, most people are looking for fun, exercise, and social life. If they compete, they try to win; but they don't expect to win all the time. However, there are elite athletes who strive to be the best in their sport. They aspire to medals, cups, and championships. Some of these elite athletes are disabled. Some have been disabled from birth and have gone on to become fine athletes anyway. Others were athletes before they became disabled and returned to sports afterward.

There are many competitions for disabled athletes, but the most important is the Paralympic Games. The Paralympics are to disabled athletes what the Olympics are to able-bodied athletes. The first Paralympic Games were held in Rome in 1960. They have been held every four years since then, usually in the same city as the Olympics. This connection with the Olympics is intended to show that disabled athletes are world-class athletes who happen to have disabilities. In 1992, the Paralympic Games were held in Barcelona, Spain, three weeks after the Olympic Games. More than 3,100 disabled athletes from 94 countries competed for 12 days in 16 sports including swimming, basketball, fencing, tennis, table tennis, weight lifting, archery, shooting, and volleyball. The athletes lived in the Olympic Village, competed in the Olympic stadiums, and took part in similar opening and closing ceremonies. They won medals and set new records. Their victories showed what disabled people can do.

At the opposite end of the scale from elite athletes are people who only watch sports on television—or who don't even do that. They prefer hobbies to sports. Most hobbies are easily accessible to people with disabilities, and there are many adaptive aids for those who have problems with their hands or vision. Occupational therapists can suggest aids to make many hobbies possible. Mail-order catalogs list playing-card shufflers and holders; large print, Braille, and magnetic games; page turners, magnifiers, and grasping aids. Magazines for the disabled often suggest simple devices that can be made at home. And computers are opening up many new possibilities.

The list of possible hobbies is almost endless: painting, needlework, carpentry, photography, writing poetry, performing magic, collecting sports cards, etc. Hobbies need not be done alone. Community centers, Ys, and schools of continuing education offer classes in everything from Chinese cooking to music appreciation to raising tropical fish. There are bridge, chess, and backgammon clubs for meeting other players, and computer networks where disabled people can communicate with others who share their interests.

For some people the ideal recreation is not doing things but going places. The Americans with Disabilities Act (ADA) says that public places, hotels, and transportation must be accessible to the disabled. Although the ADA went into effect in January 1992, not all public places have yet complied with the law. Some restaurants, theaters, and sports arenas are accessible; some are not.

Some hotels and motels have installed ramps and curb cuts; some haven't. Sometimes an accessible entrance is hidden around the side or back without any sign pointing to it. New elevator buttons have raised numbers for the blind and are placed low for wheelchair users; old elevators can be a problem. There are accessible lavatories on 767 and some 747 airplanes, but none on older planes. It will be some time before people with disabilities can travel without running into any barriers. Meanwhile, they have to check out accessibility if they want to go across town to a rock concert or across the country to the Grand Canyon.

However, with some planning, disabled people can travel almost anywhere. They can sightsee in London or Paris, cruise tropical waters, visit local resorts, or go camping. There are special tours for the disabled, or they can join a regular tour if they let the tour know in advance about any special needs. If they prefer independent travel, there are travel agents who specialize in setting up vacations for people with disabilities. Or they can make their own plans. Then it is time for a change of scenery, new experiences, a chance to make new friends, relaxation, fun, and adventure.

For people who like the great outdoors, all 242 parks, recreation areas, wildlife refuges, and historic sites of the National Parks system are accessible to wheelchair visitors. The National Parks also have audio programs and Braille markers for blind visitors as well as captioned introductory programs for the deaf or hard-of-hearing. The Golden Access Passport gives disabled people free admission to the parks and half-off fees for camping, boat launching, etc.

For those who prefer excitement to nature, theme parks are a popular destination. Disney World is particularly well set up for disabled visitors. (It received the U.S. Architectural and Transportation Barriers Compliance Award.) Disney World's Disabled Guest Guidebook tells what is available. Most rides, attractions, restaurants, and shops are accessible, as are the hotels. Visitors can remain in their wheelchairs for some attractions, but must be helped in and out for others. There are audio cassette park tours and loans of tape players to help blind visitors get around.

For people who are looking for both nature and excitement, several organizations offer wilderness trips for the disabled. There is white-water rafting down the Colorado River, kayaking to a glacier in the Yukon, horseback trekking in Yellowstone National Park, camping in the Rocky Mountains, dogsledding in Minnesota, climbing in the Grand Canyon, and more. Some wilderness trips are run by disabled people for disabled people. These are usually accompanied by able-bodied helpers. Other trips integrate people with and without physical disabilities. They all offer challenge and adventure.

Wilderness adventures get disabled people out of their everyday lives, challenge them, and show them what they can do. The same can be said of all travel, sports, and hobbies. When people become disabled and have to learn to live with what they can't do, they may feel that they have lost control of their lives. Sports, hobbies, and travel are more than ways to have fun. They are also ways for disabled people to see what they *can* do and to take charge of their lives.

CHAPTER 10

Who Am I?

Christy Brown became a writer in spite of being born with cerebral palsy and having only the use of his left foot. When the actor Daniel Day-Lewis prepared for his role as Christy Brown in the film *My Left Foot,* he used a wheelchair and had someone lift him into cars and feed him in restaurants. Even though people recognized the actor and knew what he was doing, something strange happened. He was treated like a child. People talked around him as if he was invisible. Waiters asked the person feeding him if Daniel was enjoying his meal. This treatment made him furious— a feeling many disabled people share.

When Mr. Day-Lewis finished the film and abandoned the wheelchair, he was again treated like a worthwhile adult. Unfortunately, people with real disabilities can't walk away from their wheelchairs, drop their white canes, or stop shaking and stuttering. When they are treated like second-class citizens, they may get angry as Mr. Day-Lewis did. Or they may doubt their own worth.

Everyone's self-image (how they see themselves) and self-esteem (how good they feel about themselves) are affected by the way the world relates to them. If people are treated as if they are worthwhile, they feel good about themselves. If others treat them with contempt or avoid them, they tend to feel inferior or defective.

Small children whose loving families accept them for who they are have good self-esteem. Because their families encourage them, they reach out and try new things. If they succeed, they develop greater self-confidence. They can accept failing because it doesn't make them feel less worthwhile. They also tend to be outgoing and friendly. Because their families love and accept them, they expect other people to like them, too. This expectation usually comes true—for able-bodied children.

Many children who are born with disabilities don't see themselves as different until they leave the protection of their families and go to school. It comes as a painful shock if their classmates tease or ignore them. They often feel that the rejection is their fault, and they start to see their disability as "bad." Studies show that teens who have been disabled since birth have lower self-esteem than able-bodied teens. Years of being regarded as different or inferior make it hard for them to feel "I'm okay."

Teens are particularly sensitive to what other people think of them because they are not sure of themselves. They are growing from children into adults. They are adjusting to their maturing bodies, forming relationships with the opposite sex, trying out new roles, and preparing to take their places in the adult world. Change is rarely smooth and easy. Teens ask themselves: Am I attractive? Do people approve of me? Do I measure up? Will I be successful? Their self-esteem depends on the answers to these questions.

One way to judge yourself is to look at other people. If you fit in, you're okay. If you are different, you have a problem. You can deal with the problem of being different by being ashamed, by trying to fit in, or by believing that you are right and the others are wrong. Most teens are comfortable looking and acting like everyone else in small ways and saving being different for important issues. Disabled teens don't usually have that luxury because they look different.

Members of So Fed Up, a disabled students' club, held a meeting to explain their feelings to the rest of the school. Some of the things they said were: "I was lonely as a kid. I didn't have friends because I couldn't run or keep up with the games." "I have a good sense of humor, so people like me. But I don't always feel like being funny." "Where I come from, men are supposed to be strong. If I'm not strong, how can I be a man?" "When you're disabled, you have to keep proving that you're not helpless. You can't let down sometimes like normal people can." "What do you mean by 'normal'? I'm disabled, but my body feels normal to me." They all said, "We want to belong. We want to be treated like everyone else."

When able-bodied teens are injured or become chronically ill, every part of their lives is affected. They may have to switch schools or plan for a different career. They often must give up favorite activities and find new ways of having fun. Their families may overprotect them or push them to do things before they are ready. Some of their friends disappear, and they may have trouble making new ones. Schoolmates may insist on helping them when they don't need help or look away in embarrassment when they do. Ignorant strangers may give them a taste of the treatment Daniel Day-Lewis suffered.

The practical reality of living as a disabled person often further undermines self-esteem that has already been damaged by what the injury or illness has done to the body. People's sense of who they are is closely tied to the way their bodies look and work. When they no longer feel attractive or when they cannot depend on their bodies to do what they have always done, their self-esteem drops.

We live in a society that values beauty and strength. Women should be young, pretty, slim but sexy, and fun to be with. Men should be tall, handsome, and athletic and hold high-paying jobs. Call these standards unrealistic, sexist, or just stupid; but everyone is affected by them to some extent. Fat, intelligent girls and short, musical boys may feel inadequate. So, too often, do people with disabilities.

The newly disabled are often ashamed of what has happened to them. They may be uncomfortable in public, imagining that people are staring at them or trying not to stare. (Sometimes it isn't their imagination.) They may be embarrassed by keeping others waiting while they struggle up the stairs on their crutches or refuse to eat in a restaurant because they must have their food cut up. In a world of healthy people, those who are sick may be ashamed of looking pale or having their hair fall out. They may hide their illnesses if they can or say they are getting better. They may feel guilty about being sick, as if it is somehow their fault.

Accident victims often feel guilty if there was any possibility the accident could have been avoided—or sometimes even if it couldn't. When Steven overheard his mother saying she'd always been afraid something would happen to him, he thought she blamed him. And he blamed himself. If only he'd looked where he was going, he could easily have steered around the fishing line. The secret guilt gnawed at him.

He kept it secret until the afternoon Trisha told the support group, "I always wore my seat belt. Always. Except the one time I needed it. It's like it's my fault I got hurt. Like I did this to myself." Then Steven was able to share his own guilt. It was a relief to talk about it.

Carmen listened to Trisha and Steven blaming themselves. Then she said, "Maybe you could've been more careful. But the only way to be sure you'll never have an accident is to spend your life hiding under your bed. Then the house could get hit by lightening. So it's dumb to feel guilty."

Maurice said, "Maybe it is dumb, but sometimes you can't help it. My father left when I got sick. He'd left us before, but this time he didn't come back. My mother says he can't take responsibility, so he ran away when the going got tough. But I keep feeling it's my fault. If I hadn't gotten sick, the family would still be together."

The others assured him that he wasn't to blame for getting cancer or for his father's running out on the family. Then Yoko said slowly, "I think Maurice knows that—in his head, at least. But it's hard not to feel that you did something wrong. Otherwise, why did this happen to you? Why did it happen to me?" No one had an answer.

When people become disabled, they also become more dependent on those around them. They are often ashamed of needing help because our society values independence. It tends to assume that people who can't make it on their own are not really trying. If you are poor, you must be lazy. If you don't hear, you are not paying attention. If you are learning disabled, you aren't trying hard enough.

The ideal adult in our society is completely independent. Children are taken care of; grown-ups are supposed to care for themselves. And teens want to be grown-up. When they are disabled and they need help getting dressed or going to the bathroom or getting around, they feel like babies again. Being sick or hurt makes everyone feel like a child to some extent, but teens are particularly ashamed of such feelings.

Many people who have disabilities feel they have to work harder than others to be independent and prove that they are worthwhile. As the Harris Poll showed, American society offers the disabled two roles: brave superhero or pathetic cripple. Neither role is realistic, but some disabled people try to be superheroes rather than be pitied. They are always cheerful and hard-working. They take all obstacles in their stride as they continually strive to overcome the limits of their disability.

If disabled people set life goals for themselves that are too high, they feel like failures when they don't live up to them. Even if they manage to pull off the superhero role, they may feel that they are fooling the rest of the world. It becomes difficult for them to ask for or accept help for fear of showing that they have weaknesses like everyone else.

Everyone needs some help at some time, and most people aren't very good at asking for it. They may have trouble expressing their needs. Or they may expect too much or too little from others. Some people feel they should be able to do everything alone. Others give up at the first obstacle. These attitudes can cause problems when people become disabled and need additional help. A more realistic attitude is to ask oneself honestly: How much help do I really need? Who can I depend on to help me? How does being dependent on others make them feel about me? How does it make me feel about myself?

In the days and weeks after an injury or the onset of an illness, people do their best to deal with what has happened to them. They deny or mourn, cry or rage or pray, work at getting better or give up, or go through some mixture of these reactions. As the weeks and months pass, they learn to live with the damage to their bodies or with the uncertainty of their illness. They work out a balance between independence and needing help. Exactly what kind of balance depends on what they were like before.

People who have always been very independent will take pride in how well they cope with their disability. Their self-esteem grows when they do something for themselves. They see every independent move as a victory and every need for help as a defeat. Offers of assistance upset them or make them angry. At the opposite pole are people who see help as love. Their self-esteem is tied to having people do things for them. Help makes them feel loved and cherished and seems to make up for what they have suffered. So they sit back and expect their family and friends to take care of them. Most people fall somewhere between these extremes. Those who make the best adjustment do what they reasonably can for themselves and are also able to ask for help when they need it.

Helpers often have problems of their own that make it harder for the disabled to discover what they can and should do for themselves. In trying to ease their own grief and misery, families may become overprotective and discourage trying anything new or any venturing out of the safety of the home. Parents may coddle their sick or injured child, treating a ten-year-old as if he were five or a sixteen-year-old as if she were still ten. Grandparents and other relatives may fuss or give unwanted advice. Close friends may be so eager to help that the disabled person may feel unable to ever repay them. Or friends may hang back for fear of doing the wrong thing. And strangers can be surprisingly insensitive. Helpers' attitudes can interfere with disabled people's struggle to take charge of their lives. They can undermine self-esteem.

One session of the support group turned into a round of horror stories about being "helped." Trisha complained about going to a restaurant with her family and propping her crutches against the wall. Later, wanting to go to the bathroom, she reached for her crutches. They were gone. "My mother ran all over the place looking for them. It turned out that the waiter had put them away for 'safe-keeping.' Without telling me!"

Steven said, "At least it was just your crutches. They can't move *you* around. Last week, going into school, I thought I'd left my math book on the bus. I stopped at the foot of the ramp to look through my backpack. All of a sudden, I was being pushed up the ramp at 60 miles an hour. And the guy who did it was so proud of doing a good deed. How would he feel if he stopped at the bottom of the stairs and someone picked him up and carried him to the top?"

Yoko said, "He'd be scared. Like I am when somebody grabs my arm and steers me across the street. Why don't they ask if I need help first?"

Carmen answered, "I think it's because they only see that you're blind. They don't really see *you*. There was this cartoon about a girl in a wheelchair. Two other girls ask her, 'Do we call you handicapped or disabled?' And she says, 'Call me Charlotte.'"

Able-bodied people often do not know how to help someone who is disabled. So they either turn away and let the disabled person struggle, or rush in and take over. It doesn't occur to them to ask Steven, "Do you want a push up the ramp?" or to ask Yoko, "Would you like to take my arm to cross the street?" One of the reasons they don't ask is that—as Carmen pointed out—they are relating to the disability instead of the person. This attitude creates problems for disabled people beyond the "help" that frustrates them. When others see only their disabilities, it is hard for them to think of themselves as whole people. And when others intrude into their personal space or push them around as if they were pieces of furniture, disabled people feel less in control of their lives.

Having control over one's life is vital to everyone's self-esteem. We start to take control almost as soon as we are born. The hungry child cries and is fed. He learns to walk and toddles across the room to grab what he wants. He learns to talk and says "No." With each skill learned, children become more able to make choices. Learning to read, to cross the street, and to ride a bike are steps that lead to driving a car, applying for a job, and deciding who (or if) to marry.

When an illness or accident destroys some of their abilities, people may feel that they are no longer in charge of their lives, especially if they are forced to give up activities that they value and that build their self-esteem. The person who must leave his or her job, the athlete who can no longer compete, the music lover who can't hear the notes—all may feel helpless and worthless. People with chronic illnesses often don't make plans or take on long-term projects because they never know when the disease will make it impossible for them to carry through. It seems easier not to arrange a picnic or train for a career than to face the disappointment if sickness interferes. But giving up valued activities makes them feel at the mercy of the disease.

An important goal of rehabilitation is to teach people to take control of their lives again. The rehab center offered Trisha, Steven, Christopher, Carmen, Maurice, and Yoko physical therapy, occupational therapy, and vocational counseling to strengthen their bodies, teach them new skills, and help them plan for the future. Steven was fitted for leg braces. It felt wonderful to be on his feet again, and he practiced until he could use the braces for short distances as an alternative to his wheelchair. Maurice got his new arm. Before he left OT, he could turn the pages of a book with the hook. Carmen had breathing therapy to help head off asthma attacks. Trisha got rid of the crutches and learned to walk without limping. After vocational counseling, Yoko began a computer program, and Chris applied to an out-of-town college.

Going to the support group at the same time let them sort out what was possible for them and what wasn't. The group helped them accept their limitations without feeling helpless or worthless. It encouraged them to make the most of the skills and talents they did have. It taught them that they didn't have to be ashamed of being disabled or try to be superhuman to make up for it.

Although the support group was part of their rehabilitation, many of the issues were the same ones they would be dealing with if they were able-bodied. All teens have to find out who they are, what they are good at, and what they want to do with their lives. They have to learn to see themselves clearly and to like what they see. The process is just harder for teens who have disabilities.

CHAPTER 11
Families

When a teen has a serious accident, his or her parents (or guardian) are legally responsible for their child's welfare. They must consult with the doctors and give their consent for all tests, treatments, or surgery. They must pay the medical and hospital bills or arrange for the bills to be paid by their insurance or medicaid. Most parents go far beyond their legal responsibilities. Other things in their lives are put on hold while they do everything in their power to help their child get better and feel better. They visit the hospital as often as possible, bringing magazines, snacks, and clean pajamas. They comb tangled hair, sponge sweaty backs, and try to be cheerful and consoling. Parents usually act in a similar way when a teen becomes seriously ill. They devote themselves to finding out what is wrong and what can be done about it.

If the injury heals well or the disease is cured, family life soon returns to normal. The teen returns to school, and the parents start thinking about things besides their child's health. But when a teen is left with a disability or chronic illness, his or her parents continue in the caretaker role. While this may be necessary, it also creates problems.

Growing up means becoming more and more independent. Newborn babies are completely dependent on their parents. As they grow from babies into children, they gradually learn to take care of themselves. The teen years are a bridge between childhood and adulthood. Teens are preparing to support themselves and to build families of their own. They spend time with friends, date, get an education, and train for a job or career. They assert their independence, questioning their parents' ideas and insisting on making their own decisions and mistakes.

Becoming an adult is never easy, but it is more difficult for disabled teens. It is hard for them and their families to separate the places where they must be dependent from where they can and should be on their own. When teens need physical help, their parents may also make decisions for them as if they were still children. Teens who have been disabled since birth usually take longer than able-bodied teens to learn to make their own choices, to take control of their own lives, and to become as independent as possible. Sometimes they remain emotionally dependent on their families forever. Able-bodied teens who were well on their way to becoming independent before they became disabled may become dependent again.

Everyone is dependent on other people to some extent. We depend on bus drivers to get us to school and work, on the police to protect us, and on our families to give us love and support. When people become sick or disabled, they usually turn to their families for help with things they can't do for themselves. Although most families are willing to help, they may have trouble knowing how much help the disabled person really needs or wants. They may do too much or too little. When the person with the disability is a teen and the helpers are his or her parents, they often do too much. Disabled teens and their parents often slip back into childhood roles.

Each member of a family has his or her own role, and these roles vary from family to family. In some families, the man's role is to earn the money while the woman runs the house and raises the children. In others, both parents hold jobs and share family responsibilities. Among single-parent families, the second parent can be absent or very involved with the children. Some children are given responsibility from an early age, while others are babied until they marry. Often one child is assigned the role of the family baby, or the responsible child, or the bright or beautiful or clumsy one. But whatever a person's role has been, it changes when he or she becomes disabled. Parents and children and brothers and sisters have to work out new family roles.

Since people feel comfortable in the roles they are used to, they often try to cope with a disability by going deeper into an accustomed role or returning to an earlier role. Disabled teens and their families may go back to the way they acted when the teen was a child. Sometimes parents become overprotective, sometimes teens regress to childish behavior, and sometimes the two go hand in hand.

Trisha had always been the family baby. Whenever she was in any kind of trouble, her parents or sisters stepped in to protect her. So it was natural for them to take care of her after her accident and to try to make life easier for her. Trisha responded by whining and complaining. Her family comforted and consoled her. She became more babyish, and they indulged her more. When she insisted she couldn't dress herself or get around on her crutches, they did everything for her. This behavior went on until the doctor convinced them that the best way to take care of Trisha was to force her to take care of herself. At first that made Trisha angry, but eventually she learned to be more independent. And she discovered that solving her own problems made her feel good about herself.

Christopher's mother had worried and fussed over him when he was younger because he was all she had. As he grew older, she realized that if she loved him, she had to let him go. So she agreed to his going to an out-of-town college. But when Chris developed MS, his mother slipped back into her old role. She worried constantly, imagining him sick and helpless 300 miles away with nobody to take care of him. She pressured him to switch to a school near home. Although Chris fought her at first, he gave in after his second attack. He let his mother keep him home and watch over him.

It is easy for parents and newly disabled teens to slip into earlier roles. Parents may take over, give more help than is needed, intrude on their child's privacy, or ignore his or her wishes. They may do everything their way, acting as if a physical disability cancels out the teen's ability to make decisions. Disabled teens may play along, either because they want to or because they are afraid not to. At any age, a person who needs help from others tends to do what the helpers want. And being a child again can be very tempting.

Sometimes, this return to childhood roles is temporary. As teens and their parents learn to live with the disability, they work out new roles. Trisha did. She learned that being the youngest in the family didn't have to mean being the family baby. And after a year at the local college, Christopher and his mother talked again about his going away. Chris said that being on his own was even more important to him now. It was bad enough knowing he could have a serious attack anytime without hanging around waiting for it. He wanted to do as much as he could for as long as he could. He and his mother finally agreed on Chris's going away to his first-choice college—providing he called home regularly so his mother wouldn't worry.

Going back to the old parent-child role is not the only way of coping with a disability. A person can go deeper into any accustomed role. The family worrier will find more to worry about. The optimist will look on the bright side and hope for the best. Maurice, who had a chip on his shoulder before he developed cancer, got touchier and more suspicious after he lost his arm. Carmen's way of handling trouble had always been to laugh it off, so her jokes kept the support group grinning. Yoko was a Buddhist, a religion that preaches acceptance. She struggled to accept the loss of her eyesight calmly.

Some accustomed roles cannot be maintained because the disability makes it impossible for the person to do the things he or she did before. Other family members must mow the lawn or cook the meals or earn the money. These practical changes affect the way the family members see themselves and one another.

Steven's injury changed his relationship with his younger brother, Paul. Steven had always been the strong, daring big brother. Paul looked up to Steven, while Steven protected and encouraged Paul. Steven put a stop to it when Paul was being bullied at school. He taught Paul to do skateboard tricks. He gave him tips about girls. Now the tables were turned. Paul took over Steven's old chores. He helped Steven with his exercises and into the shower afterward. Paul said he was glad to do it. But it made him uncomfortable to have Steven depend on him. Steven didn't like the switch in roles either, but he, too, pretended it didn't bother him.

Because they didn't want to hurt each other's feelings, neither Steven nor his brother talked about how they felt. And their parents acted as if there wasn't any problem. This is a common situation in loving families. Although the disability changes the whole family's lives, they pretend that the changes and sacrifices don't bother them. They act happy and cheerful to protect one another. If the disabled person seems unhappy, the rest of the family rushes in to make him or her feel better.

Steven's parents did everything in their power to make him happy. Knowing how important speed and mobility were to him, they took a loan on the house to buy him an expensive race chair and a car with hand controls. Steven was thrilled and grateful. He told them they were the best parents in the world. And he meant it. But he wished he didn't have to act happy for them all the time. He asked the support group, "How can I say to them, 'You guys are great. You've done so much for me. I don't know how I could've gotten through all this without you. But couldn't you let me be unhappy sometimes?'"

The group urged Steven to tell his parents exactly that. When he did, he was surprised and relieved to hear them say that they admired him for being so brave, but they'd still be proud of him if he let down sometimes. It turned out that he was hiding his discouragement and misery from his parents, and they were hiding theirs from him. Then Paul said that Steven and their parents always acted as if nothing bothered them, so he was ashamed of himself when he felt bad. They all agreed that it was reasonable to be unhappy sometimes and that they'd feel better if they didn't have to hide their feelings.

Nobody can read minds. Even loving families like Steven's need to talk honestly about what they feel and what they need from one another. Often the disabled person has to open the subject because the rest of the family is afraid of upsetting him or her if they bring it up.

When a sickness or injury changes people's usual routines and relationships, they often stop and think about what is important to them. Some families are drawn closer together. When Steven and Paul were younger, their father taught them to play ball and ride bikes and swim. He coached Steven's Little League team. But when Steven dropped out of Little League (he never liked organized activities) and Paul wasn't interested in joining, their father coached other boys while Steven and Paul went off with their friends. When Steven became a teenager, he and his father argued over things like taking out the garbage and coming in on time. His father wanted Steven to be more responsible. Steven wanted to be free to have a good time.

After the accident, Steven's father helped him with his morning and evening routines. They got to talking and found that they agreed more than they disagreed. Before the accident, Steven's father rarely praised him. Now he told Steven that he admired his perseverance with his rehab. And Steven told his father how much the race chair and car and driving lessons meant to him. He asked his father to be his racing coach. When Steven entered his first race, his father and mother and brother cheered him on. When he placed sixth in his class, he gave his father's coaching the credit.

Steven's disability brought him closer to his father

because their disagreements were just the normal squabbles between teens and parents. When one member of a loving family is hurt or sick, minor conflicts are often forgotten while everyone pitches in to help. But an injury or illness doesn't cure long-term family problems. Family members who were distant or uncaring before don't suddenly become loving and giving.

Christopher's father moved to California after the divorce. He said he still loved Chris and sent money to prove it. He sent a check every month to pay for the things Chris's mother's salary didn't cover, plus extra checks for Chris's birthdays and Christmas. He offered to pay for college tuition. But he never invited Chris to California, and he was always in a rush on the phone. When Chris's mother called his father about the diagnosis, Chris couldn't help hoping it would change things. Maybe his father would fly to New York, or at least stop his mother from fussing over him. But his father just said, "Get Chris the best doctors. I'll pay for it."

An injury or illness can bring a family closer, as it did with Steven's. It can leave family problems pretty much the same, as with Christopher and his parents. Or it can break up a family. A disabled person needs a large share of a family's time and money. The money spent on medical care, special equipment, etc., often means that other family members can't afford some of the things they want. The family also takes care of the disabled person or does tasks he or she can't do, leaving less time for other activities. Families that got along well before the disability adjust to the situation. They learn to balance the disabled person's special needs with the needs of the rest of the family. Families that were in trouble before can break up under the strain.

Maurice's parents had fought for as long as he could remember. Their fights often ended with his father walking out and staying away for days. When Maurice developed cancer, his parents took out their worries on each other. The fights got worse and the separations longer. On the day Maurice's arm was amputated, his parents fought so bitterly that his father left for good. His mother blamed his father for the breakup. Sometimes Maurice blamed his father, and sometimes he blamed both of them. Sometimes he blamed himself because his sickness drove them apart. What really happened was that the marriage had been breaking up for years, and Maurice's illness was the last straw.

Whether for better or worse, every member of a family is affected when one member becomes disabled. Next we look at how teens react to a parent, grandparent, brother, or sister with a disability.

CHAPTER 12

Other Families

What effect a family member's disability has on a teen's life depends on who is disabled and what the disability is. A grandparent's disability is usually the easiest to adjust to emotionally. Everyone grows old eventually. While many people remain healthy and active into their 80s, others develop physical problems that make it hard for them to do what they used to. Teens usually see their grandparents' "attacks" or difficulty in getting around as the natural order of things. When a grandparent becomes seriously ill or can no longer take care of himself or herself, it is less of a shock than when a young person becomes disabled.

If the grandparent lives in another part of the country, teens' lives are usually not much affected. Although they may feel sad and phone or send little gifts, the responsibility for dealing with the problem falls on their parents.

Teens will have a greater feeling of loss if a grandparent who lives with them or nearby becomes sick or disabled, especially when they are used to doing things together or turning to them for advice. And in those families where a grandparent is like another parent (or perhaps the only parent), the impact can be as great as when a parent is disabled.

For many teens, a grandparent's illness or disability is the first time something bad has happened to someone they love, and that is hard to bear. They may feel threatened and insecure. Some teens react by turning away from the painful situation, but most pitch in to help. Those who do chores for disabled grandparents, or just keep them company, often find that they get to know one another better.

Sometimes a grandparent who has always been independent becomes too sick or frail to live alone. Teens often feel put upon when a grandparent moves in with them because they have to give up their rooms or "babysit." Some teens find that a closer relationship with the grandparent makes up for the inconvenience. Grandparents have time to listen. They often become teens' allies in the struggle for independence from their parents. In an argument about using the car or a later curfew, it helps to say, "Grandma agrees with me. She told me that you did it at my age."

This close bond with a grandparent is usually not possible when the disability is mental rather than physical. Although teens may love a grandparent whose mind wanders or who does strange things, they are often also embarrassed or ashamed. A girl whose grandfather had **Alzheimer's disease** (which affects memory and reasoning) refused to bring friends home because she was afraid he would walk in with his fly open and egg on his beard. Her brother stayed away whenever possible. When their parents finally decided to put the old man in a nursing home, the grandchildren were relieved. But they were also sad and guilty because they remembered their grandfather giving them candy and telling them stories when they were small.

Depending on the circumstances, a grandparent's disability may affect a teen's life a lot, a little, or hardly at all. But a **sibling's** disability always means drastic changes.

When a child is disabled by an accident or illness, parents go through emotional stages like those experienced by people who become disabled themselves. Parents suffer shock, confusion, denial, anger, guilt, and grief. Meanwhile, they have to deal with medical problems, make decisions about their child's care, and worry about how to pay for everything. Because they feel overwhelmed, they may have little time or energy to spare for their other children.

Yoko's mother remembers the months after she found out that Yoko was going blind. "I couldn't think about anything else. Miriko, my younger daughter, was taking ballet lessons, and I'd promised we'd see *The Nutcracker* for her birthday. But I was so upset about Yoko that I forgot all about the ballet. And Miriko never reminded me. She's such a good, quiet child that I almost forgot she was around. I feel bad about that now."

Paul, Steven's brother, had a different experience from Miriko. His parents involved him in everything they did for Steven. Paul worked with his father and uncle to build the porch ramp for Steven's wheelchair. He moved Steven's posters and albums into his new room. When Steven came home, Paul helped him with his exercises. Paul didn't feel ignored or left out, but he couldn't help wishing that his parents would do something for him for a change.

For a while after an accident or diagnosis, much of a family's life revolves around the disabled child. Everyday routines are reorganized for his or her special needs. The house may be altered, or the family may move. The cost of health care and equipment usually leaves less money for things the rest of the family wants. Family outings and vacations may become a thing of the past. The needs of other children may be temporarily forgotten.

Meanwhile, the siblings of the disabled child are going through the same shock and grief as their parents. They may feel guilty for being strong and healthy, or they may be afraid of something happening to them, too. Often siblings insist that nothing is bothering them because they are ashamed of their feelings or because they don't want to add to their parents' burdens. Like Paul and Miriko, they put their brother's and sister's needs ahead of their own. They may act as if they don't have any needs.

If able-bodied siblings are ignored for too long, they often become jealous of the care and attention their parents are giving the disabled child. Some jealousy between siblings is normal. All brothers and sisters have both negative and positive feelings for one another. They love one another—when they are not fighting. Sometimes they offer one another support; other times they compete. They can be jealous or unselfish, caring or angry, sympathetic or impatient, proud of the sibling or ashamed. If parents forget that their able-bodied children have needs, too, the negative feelings can get the upper hand.

Some siblings react to what they see as unfair treatment with complaints and anger. Others make trouble to get attention. If nobody notices them when they are good, they will be bad. They will fail in school or steal a car or get pregnant. Still others suppress their resentment and become overly involved in the disabled sibling's care, behaving more like parents than like brothers or sisters. Or they become superachievers to make up to their parents for what the disabled child cannot do.

Teens with a sibling who was born disabled don't face a sudden adjustment problem. They have lived with the sibling's disability for all or most of their lives and are used to the family roles it has created. But they face other problems. For one thing, they are likely to be ashamed of their brother or sister.

When a baby is born disabled, the disability is often mental. More babies are born mentally retarded than with most other birth defects put together. Brothers and sisters of mentally or emotionally disabled children are often teased by other children about their sibling's behavior. As a result, some teens are ashamed of their disabled sibling, others get upset at every imagined slur, and others become cautious about making friends. Some don't have problems with friends of the same sex, but they hide their sibling from their dates. They worry that nobody will ever want to marry them because of the sibling. If the disability is inherited, they worry about having children.

When the able-bodied teen is the oldest—especially if she is female—she usually takes the caretaker role. She acts as her sibling's teacher and protector. If the responsibility isn't too great, it will probably make her into a caring and mature person. Many teens say that having a disabled sibling has made them more tolerant of people's differences and more sympathetic to other people's needs.

However, if the responsibility is too much of a burden, a sister may be torn between her love for her sibling and her resentment at having her own needs neglected. Some teens feel that they never had a chance to be children, that they always had to worry about their sibling. They complain about getting less praise for earning A's in school than the sibling did for washing his hands. Sometimes a teen will rebel against the caretaker role she accepted earlier.

Most parents don't want to burden their healthy children, but some have little choice. A single parent caring for a disabled child along with earning a living and running a house will need more help from her able-bodied child than two parents living together. Families with money to hire outside help or who get good social services will put less pressure on the other children. Caring relatives and friends can also ease the burden.

Usually the more serious the disability, the more siblings will have to help take care of the disabled child. Children with mild physical or mental disabilities can take their normal places in the family with some help. Although a boy who uses crutches can't mow the lawn, he can do the dishes sitting on the kitchen stool. But a girl with cerebral palsy may have to be washed and dressed and fed. And severely retarded children usually need constant supervision.

Children whose parents depend on them to help care for their disabled siblings face special problems when they reach their late teens. They ask themselves: How will my parents manage if I go away to school, move out, or marry? What will happen to my sibling if my parents get sick or die? It is important for them to discuss these problems with their parents and to make plans that take everyone's needs into account.

As much as teens may be called on to help when a sibling or grandparent is disabled, the major responsibility still falls on their parents. But when a parent is disabled, family life is turned upside down. Parents usually take care of children; now the children find themselves taking care of the parent. If the disability is temporary,

teens take over some of the parent's responsibilities during the emergency. Then life goes back to normal. But
when the disability is permanent, parents and children
have to work out new roles.

Usually the healthy parent and the older children
share the tasks that the disabled parent can no longer do.
In one family where the mother is crippled by MS, she still
organizes the housework and plans the meals. The father
does the shopping and outside chores, the older daughter
cooks, the younger daughter does the laundry, and the
three of them pitch in for the occasional bouts of house-
cleaning. The house is set up so that the mother can get
around easily in her wheelchair and do as much as possible for herself. The daughter who has the late session in
high school helps her mother wash and dress in the morning. An electric scooter gives the mother the freedom to
visit neighbors or go to the doctor on her own during the
day.

This family had time to work out their roles because
the disability developed gradually. The adjustment is
harder when the disability is sudden. And single-parent
families have special problems. Most communities provide social services—visiting nurses, social workers, aids,
etc.—to help families deal with a disability. Private organizations also provide information, medical referrals, legal
help, counseling, workshops, and/or job training.

In addition to the practical problems that a parent's
disability creates, teens also face emotional problems.
While they love and sympathize with their mother or
father, they often also feel betrayed or angry because he
or she can no longer always be there for them. They feel
guilty about their negative responses and may be afraid
the parent will get worse or die. Sometimes they withdraw

from the painful situation, locking themselves in their rooms or staying away from home. More usually, they try to make up to the parent for what has happened by devoting themselves to his or her care or by being the perfect child.

An oldest daughter, particularly, may become the family "mother." Between schoolwork, housework, and taking care of her parent and the younger children, she may have little time for herself. She may be too busy to see friends or date, or she may feel guilty about leaving her parent alone while she is having a good time. It is natural for teens to give newly disabled parents all the help they can and to try not to burden them with their problems and fears. But teens also have lives of their own to lead. Eventually, they should learn to balance their own needs with the parent's needs.

The teen years are the time for gradually becoming independent from one's family. Disabled teens have problems with independence because they need their parents' help. Able-bodied teens have problems when a disabled parent needs their help. Some teens in this situation feel that the only way to become independent is to leave home. Some go to the other extreme, insisting that they are perfectly happy at home helping their parent. Others become touchy about any advice or interference: "I'm cooking. Don't tell me how much salt to use." Ideally, teens and their parents can talk to one another about what each of them really needs and work out solutions together.

Although a parent's disability creates problems, it can also bring greater understanding between parents and children. Parents discover that their children can be relied on. Children realize that their parents are human beings with strengths and weaknesses. A crisis makes people think about what is really important to them. Parents and children often discover that what is important is loving one another, and they work together to deal with the crisis.

Studies show that having a disabled person in the immediate family has both negative and positive effects on children and teens. Children with disabled siblings are more likely to be anxious, to have fewer friends, and to have conflicts with their parents. The more children and teens are pressed into the caretaker role, the more likely they are to show negative effects. Teens who have too many caretaking responsibilities tend to leave home early. However, many teens who have a disabled sibling or parent are more tolerant and more mature than others of their age. They identify with the disabled person, take pride in helping him, and rejoice in her achievements.

Why do some teens feel that having a disabled parent or sibling has made them more mature, caring, and independent, while others complain about having to grow up too soon? Surprisingly, studies show that the severity of the disability or whether it is mental or physical does not make much difference in teens' reactions. The deciding factor seems to be the way the family handles the situation. In other words, while it is not possible to keep people from becoming disabled, it is possible to keep the disability from destroying their lives and the lives of the people around them.

CHAPTER 13

Choices

B en had brought in pizza and soda because it was the last meeting of the support group, but they were all feeling a little sad. They'd become good friends over the past eight months, and this was the last time they would all be together. Trisha had finished her rehab. She was walking well now, although she limped a little when she was tired and her hip ached in damp weather. Christopher and Carmen were leaving town. Chris was going away to college, and Carmen's family was moving to Arizona, where the climate was supposed to be better for asthma. Maurice had said he might move away, too, when his parents' divorce came through. Because it was hard to say "Good-bye," the group members concentrated on eating their pizza.

Ben said, "We can talk while we eat. Since this is our last session, let's talk about choices. First, I want to say loud and clear that you always have choices. You can choose what to wear and who you like and what to do with your life and whether to keep trying. Being disabled changes some of your choices, but it doesn't deprive you of choice. You can be okay if you choose to be okay. Or if you want to sit around and moan even though the world is full of wonderful things, that's your choice. That said, I thought we'd go around the room as we did in our first session and look at some of the choices you've made since then and the choices you still have to make. Trisha, will you go first?"

Trisha hesitated. "I don't think I made any special choices. I mean, I just tried to get well."

Ben asked, "Isn't trying a choice? If I remember rightly, you didn't try very hard at the beginning."

Steven snorted.

Trisha turned on him, "Don't you dare say a word about whining!"

"You said it. I didn't. Though I have to admit you were a prize whiner. But you do whine a lot less since you started working at your rehab. Actually, once you got started, you turned out to be a pretty good worker."

Coming from Steven, whose idea of working at rehab was wearing yourself into the ground, that was quite a compliment. Pleased, Trisha said, "I guess I grew up." Then she added thoughtfully, "You know, all these months since the accident, I wanted to go back to how it was before. I figured once I was walking again, I'd forget all about it like it was a bad dream. But the accident and rehab and everything changed me, and I don't want to change back. Even though the accident was the worst thing that ever happened to me, I made it through. Maybe I did whine for a while, and maybe my family had to push me. But then I did it on my own. That makes me feel that I can depend on myself now. And I like myself better." She looked at Ben. "I guess I chose to grow up."

Ben smiled. "We don't always see what choices we're making while we're making them. That's why I asked you to look back today. Who wants to be next?"

Surprisingly, Yoko volunteered. "I'm choosing not to think of myself as Blind Yoko, just as Yoko. Even though being blind is part of my life, it isn't my whole life. It was for a long time because it was such a big job to learn to do everyday things without eyes and to get around with Blackie leading me. But now I'm ready for something new. Like singing on the school chorus. I finally got up my courage and spoke to the chorus teacher. She had me sing two songs and said I was in."

"Good for you!" Steven said. "But none of us ever thought of you as Blind Yoko. More like Yoko-Who-Sets-Us-An-Example. You're so together. I watched how you accept your disability and tried to do the same with mine. But it's an awful struggle for me."

Yoko was embarrassed by the praise. Although her natural reaction was to be silent, she wanted to help Steven. "It just takes time. I've lived with my disability longer than you have. And I had time to get used to it gradually. Nobody can accept it all at once. First you have to accept that you're really blind or crippled and it's not going away. Then little by little you accept the ways it changes your life. Finally, you stop thinking about your disability all the time because you're busy doing other things. At least, that's how it happened with me."

Steven said maybe there was hope for him yet.

Ben said that people go past their disabilities in their own ways, and he thought Steven was making a good job of it. Then he asked, "What about you, Chris?"

"I think Steven is a fighter, and we all admire him for it. That's not what you were asking, but I wanted to say it because this is our last meeting. As for me, the hardest thing to accept has been the uncertainty. Not knowing if or when I'll have another attack. So far the attacks haven't left me with a permanent disability. Just a little trouble with my balance. But maybe next time . . . "

Carmen interrupted. "If you keep thinking about what could happen to you tomorrow, you can't enjoy today."

Chris nodded. "You know how to live one day at a time. I was always a planner, and I didn't see how I could make plans if I didn't know if I'd be sick or not. It took me a long time to get to 'just do it.' I want to go away to college, so I'm going. I spoke to the doctor at the school health service and made plans with my mother for what I'd do if I had an attack at school. Then I put it out of my head. Or at least in back of my mind. I'm not thinking about MS because I'm busy choosing my new courses and buying stuff for my dorm."

Carmen imitated Ben's voice. "Good choice." They all laughed. All except Maurice.

He said, "We can talk about choices all we want in here. And we can tell one another how great we are. But it's different outside. The rest of the world doesn't think we're so great. They put all kinds of roadblocks in the way of our making choices."

Carmen said, "Maybe it used to be that way, but things are changing with the new laws and stuff. Like this A. . . . I can't think of the initials."

"ADA. It's supposed to make stores and restaurants accessible. Ask Steven how accessible they are."

Steven answered, "Some are. Most aren't. I can pop wheelies, so one step doesn't keep me out. But two steps might just as well be a locked gate."

Maurice gave Carmen an I-told-you-so look. "And ask Yoko how many Braille signs she finds. Or if she can make out those subway announcements that are supposed to tell blind people what train it is."

When Yoko shook her head, Maurice went on, "A lot of disabled people are fed up. They're organizing and picketing and protesting. They go to political conventions and demand action. They protest against telethons that make the disabled look helpless. They picket places that aren't accessible. On the news last week, I saw people in wheelchairs set up a table across the front door of a restaurant they couldn't get into. They sat there reading from a 'handicapped menu' of 'closed-to-us chili' and 'no-ramp salad.' I wanted to clap and cheer."

Carmen asked, "Why don't you join a group like that? You'd be good at protesting."

"You're kidding, but I've thought about it."

"I wasn't kidding. I'll bet Ben could put you in touch with some organization."

They looked at Ben, who said, "If you're interested, I know someone who is very active in the disability rights movement. I can give you his phone number."

Maurice said, "I'm interested."

Ben wrote down the number. Then he indicated that it was Steven's turn.

Steven said, "I have one more year of high school, and I've been thinking about what to do afterward. I asked Ben about careers in rehab. He gave me info on becoming a physical therapist, occupational therapist, recreational therapist, speech pathologist, or vocational counselor. At first I was put off by how much training they all take. The B.S.-M.S. program in physical therapy is five years, and the others are pretty much the same. Kind of overwhelming for a guy who didn't want to go to college. But I've become a pretty good student, and I'd like to give it a try. PT is my first choice. I was afraid I couldn't do it from a wheelchair until I read an article about doctors who are paraplegics, even one who's a quad. If they can do it, I can. My arms are very strong, and I'm getting good on long braces. And I could still get some return in my legs. Anyway, recreational therapy is my second choice, and that's not so strenuous."

Yoko said, "You'd be good at either one."

Trisha said with a laugh, "You'd know how to push people into doing what was good for them."

Steven smiled. Then he said seriously, "I think I would know. I'd know what they're going through because I've been through it myself. I guess the reason I want to go into rehab is to help other people the way I was helped."

Ben said, "When you apply to school, I'd be happy to give you a letter of recommendation. So would anyone else here who's worked with you." He looked at his watch. "I'm afraid our time is almost up. I just want to say. . . . "

Before he could finish, Carmen poked Trisha.

Trisha jumped up and pulled a package out from where she'd hidden it behind the desk. She held it out to Ben. "Carmen and I did the shopping, but it was Yoko's idea, and everyone chipped in."

Ben opened the package. He said he was really touched and a sweater was exactly what he needed. He said he'd think of them every time he wore it. He put the sweater right on.

He was still wearing it an hour later when the physiatrist came in to talk to him. She asked, "Isn't it hot today for a sweater?"

"This one's a present from my support group. Today was our final session. It's days like this that keep me doing this work."

"I presume this group did well?"

Ben nodded. "It always amazes me how much a group

does in less than a year. You take a bunch of ordinary kids. Some smart, some silly, some brave, some babyish. Life plays a dirty trick on them. They get sick or hurt, develop cancer or MS, go blind or smash their bones or their spines. For a while they wallow in anger or despair. But when we offer them a helping hand, they grab it and pull themselves out of their misery. They make new lives for themselves. And grow up in the process."

The physiatrist smiled. "I'm glad you're feeling so positive today because I have a problem for you. It's about the new group we're forming. I'm eager to include Scott, the boy who had the spinal tumor." She handed him Scott's folder. "As you see, the operation to remove the tumor left more paralysis than expected. Scott was devastated. He gave up and withdrew into himself. He's not making much progress in rehab because he won't try. I think a group could bring him out of his misery, but he doesn't want to join. I tried to persuade him at least to come to the first session. He just shook his head. Will you talk to him?"

Ben looked through the folder. "Scott comes to PT when Steven has OT. Let's arrange for them to meet. Steven has a better chance of changing Scott's mind about a group than either of us."

"Good idea. If anyone can persuade Scott that life must go on, it's Steven."

Ben said, "Scott will have to discover that for himself like everyone else does. Everyone—healthy or sick, disabled or able-bodied—has to choose his or her own road in life. All we can do is give them a push in the right direction."

FOR FURTHER READING

ABLE. P.O. Box 395, Dept. S, Old Bethpage, New York 11804.
Monthly newspaper for, by, and about the disabled.

Allen, Anne. *Sports for the Handicapped.* New York: Walker, 1981.
Swimming, wheelchair basketball, horseback riding, etc. With photographs.

American Automobile Association. *The Handicapped Driver's Mobility Guide.* Heathrow, Fla.: AAA, 1991.
Driving with hand controls, choosing a car, parking.

Bowe, Frank. *Handicapping America: Barriers to Disabled People.* New York: Harper and Row, 1978.
Society's attitudes toward the disabled. Barriers in housing, transportation, education, and work. Advanced reading.

Cassie, Dhyan. *So Who's Perfect!* Scottsdale, Penn.: Herald, 1984.
People with visible differences tell their own stories.

Corbet, Barry. *Options: Spinal Cord Injury and the Future.* Denver: Hershfield, 1980.
Biographies of people with spinal cord injuries who made new lives for themselves.

The Disability Rag. P.O. Box 145, Louisville, Ken.
Bimonthly magazine of the disability rights movement.

Hale, Glorya. *The New Source Book for the Disabled.* London: Heinemann, 1983.
Information on dealing with the practical problems of being disabled.

Inside MS. 205 East 42nd St., New York, New York 10017.
Magazine of the National Multiple Sclerosis Society.

Jevne, Ronna, and Alexander Levitan. *No Time for Nonsense.*
    San Diego: LuraMedia, 1989.
    *A self-help book for seriously ill people. Practical, inspir-
    ing, and funny.*

Lunt, Suzanne. *A Handbook for the Disabled.* New York:
    Scribners, 1982.
    *Guide to clothes, living aids, driving aids, sports, and
    travel for the disabled.*

Maddox, Sam. *Spinal Network.* Boulder, Col.: Spinal Network,
    1987.
    Resource book for the wheelchair community.

Meyer, Donald, Patricia Vadasy, and Rebecca Fewell. *Living
    with a Brother or Sister with Special Needs.* Seattle:
    University of Washington Press, 1985.
    *Aimed at elementary through junior-high-school students
    who have disabled brothers or sisters.*

Murphy, Robert. *The Body Silent.* New York: Holt, 1987.
    *An anthropologist discusses becoming paralyzed by a
    spinal tumor. He comments on disease in our culture.
    Advanced reading.*

Pogrebin, Letty Cottin. *Among Friends.* New York: McGraw Hill,
    1987.
    *A book about friends. Who we like, why we like them, and
    what we do with them.*

Rosner, Louis, and Shelly Ross. *Multiple Sclerosis.* New York:
    Prentice Hall, 1987.
    *Diagnosis, progress and treatment of MS. Coping and
    relationships.*

Sirof, Harriet. *Because She's My Friend.* New York: Atheneum,
    1993.
    *A young adult novel about the friendship between two
    girls after one of them becomes disabled in an accident.*

Spinal Cord Injury Life. 600 W. Cummings Park, Woburn, Mass.
    01801.
    *Quarterly magazine of the National Spinal Cord Injury
    Association.*

Zola, Irving K. *Ordinary Lives: Voices of Disability and Dis-
    ease.* Cambridge: Apple-wood, 1982.
    Stories, poems, and book excerpts about disability.

GLOSSARY

abduction brace: A device used after hip surgery to keep the patient from using the hip joint fully until it heals. The brace fits like a pair of hard plastic shorts.

accessible: Usable or available. The word is often applied to a restaurant, bus, or bathroom that can be used by disabled people.

activities of daily living or **ADL:** The skills of washing, dressing, feeding oneself, etc. Occupational therapists help patients learn ADLs after an injury or illness.

adaptive equipment: Devices to help a disabled person live as independently as possible. Adaptive equipment can be as simple as Velcro instead of shoelaces or as complicated as a motorized sip-and-puff wheelchair.

Alzheimer's disease: A disease of the central nervous system that strikes after age 50. It causes memory loss and affects thinking. The cause is not known, and there is no cure.

disability: A physical, mental, or emotional condition that lasts for six months or more and interferes with some of the activities of daily living.

gait training: Instruction in walking, with or without braces, crutches, or canes.

handicap: Something in a disabled person's world that keeps him or her from doing something. It can be a physical barrier like a staircase or discrimination that refuses the person a job he or she can do.

home instruction: Learning at home. Teachers go to the homes of students who are temporarily unable to go to school.

magnetic resonance imaging or **MRI:** A machine using magnetic fields to show views of the central nervous system that cannot be seen with X rays or CAT scans. The MRI helps doctors find diseases earlier and make more accurate diagnoses.

mainstream: To place disabled students in class with able-bodied students.

Multiple Sclerosis or **MS:** An unpredictable and often disabling disease of the central nervous system. It usually begins between the ages of 15 and 35.

myelin: Fatty tissue around nerves that helps them work efficiently. Some myelin becomes destroyed in multiple sclerosis.

nervous system: The brain, spinal cord, and the optic nerve make up the central nervous system. The nerves that branch out from the spinal cord to the rest of the body make up the peripheral nervous system.

neurologist: A doctor who specializes in the diagnosis and treatment of diseases of the nervous system.

occupational therapy or **OT:** A method of treating physical or mental disabilities. Occupational therapists use purposeful activities to help people overcome handicaps and lead more independent lives. OT teaches the activities of daily living and provides adaptive equipment.

paraplegic or **para:** A person whose lower body and legs are partly or completely paralyzed. A para's arms and upper body are usually not affected.

physiatrist: A doctor who specializes in the diagnosis and treatment of physical disability. His field is also called physical medicine and rehabilitation.

physical therapy or **PT:** A method of treating temporary or permanent disabilities that result from accidents or illness. Physical therapists use exercise, massage, heat, cold, and electric stimulation to help patients regain movement and to reduce pain. Gait training is an important part of PT.

pressure sore: An open sore caused by pressure on the skin. This is a problem for people confined to bed or to a wheelchair. Some pressure sores need surgery to close them.

psychologist: A specialist in behavior and mental states. Psychologists test intelligence, learning, perception, and mental health. They also do counseling and psychotherapy.

quadriplegic or **quad:** A person with some paralysis of the upper body and arms in addition to paralysis of the lower body.

regression: Acting in a way that is appropriate to an earlier stage of life. Being childish or unreasonable under stress.

rehabilitation or **rehab:** Restoring a person to health after an accident or illness or training him to lead the best and most independent life possible.

sibling: A brother or sister.

social worker: A person who helps individuals and families deal with the practical and emotional problems arising out of illness, family breakups, or poverty. Psychiatric social workers often do counseling or psychotherapy.

spasms: Muscle movements out of a person's control. Arms jerk or legs kick. Spasms are common in people with spinal cord injuries or with diseases like cerebral palsy.

spinal cord: A column of white nerve tissue that connects the brain to the rest of the body. Messages for movement start in the brain and travel down the spinal cord to the muscles. Sensations like touch, temperature, pressure, or pain travel up the cord to the brain. The spinal cord is protected by the bones of the spinal column that surround it.

spinal cord injury or **SCI:** Damage to the spinal cord that interrupts the flow of messages between the brain and the body and results in a loss of feeling and movement below the injury. In an incomplete injury, some feeling or ability to move may remain.

Stryker frame: A device used to keep the spine in line and prevent a patient with a spinal cord injury from moving.

t'ai chi or **t'ai chi chuan:** Also called Taoist yoga or Chinese shadow boxing. A system of slow, continuous exercises that increase muscle control, relax the body, and calm the mind.

transfer: Going from wheelchair to bed, chair, toilet, shower, bench, or car. If a person cannot stand at all, transfers are made by lifting the body onto the hands or using a sliding board.

Vocational Rehabilitation: A federal/state program to train people with disabilities for jobs or careers.

wheelie: Going up on the back wheels of a wheelchair with the front wheels off the ground. A person may pop a wheelie to get up a curb or may hold the position for a while to shift his or her weight in the chair.

INDEX